DRAGON'S KISS

RED PLANET DRAGONS OF TAJSS BOOK 5

MIRANDA MARTIN

GRAB MIRANDA MARTIN'S NEWSLETTER AND BE THE FIRST
TO KNOW ABOUT NEW RELEASES, DEALS AND GENERAL
ANTICS

CONTENTS

A **Dragon Hunter for me? No way.**

OLIVIA THINKS IT'S IMPOSSIBLE THAT THE OUTRAGEOUSLY TALL Zmaj with steely blue eyes would fall for her. A former data analyst, now she's just another human crash survivor on the harsh and alien desert planet. Smart, curvaceous Olivia doesn't feel like she measures up but that doesn't stop Ragnar from eyeing her luscious curves.

He's the best hunter for the Tribe, driven and single minded. Ragnar has always put the needs of his people over his own and never once regretted it, but now the dominant alpha male has his heart set on a different treasure. He'll claim and protect the voluptuous beauty no matter the costs.

Life on Tajss is hard enough but now the Tribe is on the run from the same pirates that crashed Olivia's ship. To find a new home will be a grueling journey through sandstorms and worse. She and Ragnar don't speak the same language but Olivia ends up falling for the alien dragon-man anyway, finding she might have to choose between the mate she's meant for and the people she belongs to.

Dragon's Kiss is the fifth book in the Red Planet Dragons of Tajss series! It contains barbaric alien-dragon men, action-packed struggle for survival, and hot, steamy dragon romance. Enjoy!

It began with Dragon's Baby and carries on from there!

OLIVIA

*S*topping, I wipe the sweat from my forehead and try to catch my breath.

"You okay?" Delilah asks, stepping out of the way as others continue loading our plundered transport with supplies.

"Yeah," I answer, trying my best not to gasp.

She sets down the pack she's carrying and puts a hand under my chin, pulling until I meet her eyes.

"Are you okay?" she repeats.

I'm still trying to breathe so I just shake my head. Delilah's my best friend, always has my back, and doesn't believe my bullshit. I couldn't ask for anyone better.

"I'll be fine," I say, hands on my knees and heaving for air. "Just, you know, not in the best of shape for this."

"I hear that," she says. "Here, have some water."

I drink from the offered container, grateful. It seems like all the others cast glances in my direction as they continue loading and a knot forms in my gut.

"We should get back to it," I say, pushing upright.

Delilah smiles then picks up her pack and enters the

transport. I walk back to the supply room and grab another pack. When I come out, Lana is standing nearby. She's everything I wish I was. Curvy, but not too much, with beautiful auburn hair. Much classier than my own shocking red. She tans too, which must be nice. Curse of being redheaded is I'm fair skinned, which means I'm burnt to a crisp.

Yup, I'm totes jealous.

I wish I could be that hot. I've got the full breasts, but they're too full. I've got the hips for sure, but too much of them. I've got everything she has but just too much of it. Shaking my head, I move past her towards the transport but as I do, I catch her conversation. I don't understand what she's saying, but she's very animated about it.

Lana is the only one who can talk to the aliens. She says they're called Zmaj. What a strange word that is, but what should I expect? They're aliens. All of them are over seven feet tall with broad shoulders and flexing, sexy chests exposed to the sun. They're the natives of this planet. Dragon-men is what us girls are calling them. It's fitting. They each have wings, a long, thick tail and scales. I even saw one of them breathe fire!

One of them, Ragnar, damn he's good looking. Serious hotness there. He's the one Lana is so animatedly talking to. I slow down, not to listen in, just to enjoy the view. He's tall, like they all are, but he has this sandy red hair on his head and the colors of his scales are tan with reddish tones to them. When he moves his arms in response to what Lana is saying his over-sized pecs flex and bounce. I swear you could drown in my panties right now.

It's been a long time since our ship crashed here and even longer since I've scratched that itch. I dated, sure, but nothing serious or for long. Sooner or later I would have married and had kids because that's the way it worked on our generation ship.

"Olivia!" Astrid exclaims as she bumps into me. She's carrying a huge load of supplies, so big that she can't see over it. Guess that's why she ran into me lolly-gagging.

Astrid is tall and really buff. I don't know what her job was on the ship but it had to be something physical. She's like a body-building amazonian goddess or some shit. She's the opposite extreme from Lana and her curves, but they're both hot as shit, and then there's my out of shape ass.

"Sorry," I say, stepping to one side.

"Just hurry up, would you?" she mutters, walking by.

The pack I had picked up is digging into my shoulders and getting rid of it seems like the best idea right now. It hurts enough to force me to tear my gaze away from Ragnar and as I turn, the hairs on the back of my neck rise. Ragnar is staring past Lana at me. My cheeks burn hot, my stomach churns, and my chest constricts.

Did he see me looking at him?

I want to crawl under a rock and hide. There's nowhere to go so I rush ahead and enter the moderate safety of the transport. Being out of the sun is a relief too, so I drop my pack on a rack and take a minute to let my heart rate settle down. How could I have let him see me staring? I know he has to have seen. My luck is the worst.

Penelope walks in carrying a small box. She's thin, too thin really, with blond hair and the most brilliant green eyes.

"You okay?" she asks, seeing me standing around trying to hide.

"Yeah," I say, feeling even worse that this is the second time in a row someone has felt the need to see if I'm okay. "Just catching my breath."

"Okay," Penelope says, turning and walking out again.

I can't stay here, I have to pull my weight. Though it's not like I asked for this. Well, on that note none of us did. None of it at all. First, we were attacked by space pirates, then we crash landed on this inhospitable, hot as fuck desert planet. Then the pirates that crashed our ship captured Delilah and I while we were gathering wood at a nearby oasis.

As if life wasn't hard enough already, adding space pirate dicks was just unnecessary. They're ugly bastards and scary too. Being captured turned out okay because they'd captured Lana and another Zmaj, Astarot, first which opened up a whole new world. Lana isn't from our part of the shipwreck. She was in a different section of the ship when it crashed into the atmosphere and broke apart. There are more survivors than we knew about. Great, that's be awesome news if they weren't somewhere so far away. Lana says her people are living in the ruins of a city.

Then there's Astarot. When Delilah and I first saw him; seven feet tall, scales, wings, tail and all I don't think we were unjustified in being worried he wanted to eat us. He looks like a freaking dragon, what else were we supposed to think? Lucky us, he didn't want to eat us. Though he might want something else, but then, I could only wish, huh? It turns out our races are... compatible. It didn't take long to see that Astarot and Lana were an item, and a hot one at that.

I've made it back to the staging cavern where all the supplies wait to be loaded.

"Can you carry that one?" Bailey asks, pointing to a pack that looks like it might weigh as much as I do.

"Maybe?" I answer.

Bend at the knees, use your back.

Grabbing it I heft, pull, then strain and get it off the ground. The pack has two handles to hold and I can only take baby steps. My back is screaming at me for putting this much pressure on it. Why the hell did Bailey ask me to carry this instead of Astrid! My arms shake with effort. I'm pushing through on willpower alone, making my way out of the room into the valley and up the slope out, one step at a time.

Think about something else. Push aside the pain, ignore the muscles trembling.

Astarot fighting.

Mmmm, yeah that's nice. Damn those Zmaj are sexy beasts!

He and Lana led the way after our escape from the pirates that captured us. Watching him fight was exciting, an explosive display of skill and strength. After we escaped, though, we were wandering the red desert wastes of rolling dunes and rocky outcroppings. I don't think anyone knew which way to go.

Then we met Ragnar. Astarot doesn't hold a candle to Ragnar's shimmering, roped muscled perfection.

My knees shake as I struggle to pull the pack up higher on my back. Focus. Pull, good. One step, now another. Sweat is pouring into my eyes. Blinking to clear my blurry vision, the weight lifts away.

Ragnar is towering over me, looking down as he shakes his head. He's holding the pack out to the side, one-handed like it's nothing. He says something that sounds like a long string of S's.

"What?" I ask, placing my hand on my hip.

He shakes his head, says something else in Zmaj that sounds like more hissing.

"I can handle it!" I say, my voice cracking.

My skin is burning and not just from the sun, people have stopped what they're doing to stare at us. Great, just what I wanted. Ragnar moves the pack up and down, still holding it one handed, and it looks like he's hefting its weight to show off how strong he is.

"Fine!" I yell, turning my back on him.

Staring straight ahead I march down to the room where

the rest of the supplies are, ignoring the stares and whispers. I look like an idiot. Of course he's stronger than I am! Ragnar's what, three or four times my size? The way the muscles rippled under the scales of his chest was just... NO! I'm not thinking about that. He embarrassed me.

Stepping into the cool room, I stop and take a moment to breathe. I handled that so damn wrong. It took me by surprise and I already feel like I'm barely pulling my weight. I'm not as fit as everyone else, obviously. I'm an analyst, but how the fuck does that help me on this desert hell? Answer, it doesn't. There's no use for someone who's main skill was sitting in a cubicle and studying patterns in numbers.

Tears well up in my eyes and I can't help myself. Footsteps are approaching and damn it, I don't want anyone to see me crying. Wiping at my eyes I inhale deeply. I can do this. I'm strong enough, good enough, nothing can stop me unless I let it. One more breath and a final wipe at my eyes then I walk into the room where Bailey is waiting.

"Make it?" she asks.

"Yeah," I answer, leaving out Ragnar's help.

"Damn, you're impressive. I figured we'd need at least two people to haul that."

Fuck my life, now she tells me! She's not looking up from her work though so I try to let it go. Two people and I was carrying it by myself. No wonder it was so damn hard. It wasn't for Ragnar though, he held it one handed like it was nothing. The muscles of his arms flexing as they curled, bulging and so strong, how good would they feel wrapped around me?

No, no, no, I think, shaking my head.

"What else needs to go?" I ask, looking around the nearly empty space.

"That's it, I don't think we can fit any more on the transport anyway," she says.

"Okay," I say. "Good. I can't wait to get back home."

Home. When did I start thinking of the wreckage of our ship as home?

"Me too," Bailey says. "They're going to flip when we bring back the Zmaj, aren't they?"

"I don't know what to expect."

Bailey puts an arm over my shoulders and gives me a motherly hug then we walk out into the valley. The activity is dying down and most everyone has gathered in the center of the box formed by the crevasse walls. Lana is standing by the way out, she and Astarot are talking to the Commander.

The Commander is the leader of the Zmaj who live in this valley, which is apparently a strange thing to Astarot. Lana gave us the down and dirty in brief. The planet used to have technology but then there was some intergalactic war they call the devastation. It killed almost all the Zmaj, leaving only a handful of males who went off to be alone and wait to die.

The war was over control of the supply of a plant called epis. It only grows here and has all kinds of properties that make it covetable. All I know is that it makes the heat not suck so bad, so I take it, like all the other humans. The only downside is it's really addictive, like die if you stop taking it addictive. It means leaving Tajss is impossible, we'll never get rescued by Earth.

Besides, what do we know of Earth now? All I know about it is what I've read in books and seen in the entertainment vid library the ship used to have. Thinking of that.... Dragon-men. Hmm, Game of Thrones much? Oh what I wouldn't give to be Daenerys riding my dragon...

No! I yell at myself, tearing my eyes off Ragnar who's walking towards me. *Oh, damn it, he's coming.*

Ragnar stops in front of me and my breath catches in my chest. The way the sunlight glints off of the scales of his massive, muscled chest is just too much. Craning my neck so I can look up at him, his thin, beautiful lips curve into what must be a smile. He says something and damn I don't care what it means my knees are weak.

He motions with his hands, trying to communicate, but I don't care what he's saying. I'm basking in the sexy he exudes and the steely blue brilliance of his eyes. His mouth moves, more sounds, then his wings rustle and I blink fast, trying to focus.

"He wants to know if you're okay?" Lana asks, coming up from somewhere.

"Huh?" Smart reply Olivia, good thinking, I berate myself.

"He's asking if you're okay," Lana repeats.

Shaking my head to clear it I turn and look at her, then back at Ragnar. Swallowing hard, I nod then smile. Lana says something to Ragnar. Stabbing, acidic jealousy burns in my stomach. What I wouldn't give to talk to him! I want to know what he's saying too. He says something then they're talking back and forth. The Zmaj tongue is fast and filled with soft sounds and hisses. It seems much faster than Common.

"Good," Lana says, looking back. "He's glad you weren't hurt."

"Hurt?" I ask. "Doing what?"

"When he came to help you, he thought you were doing too much?" She tilts her head, looking unsure of her words.

"Too much?" I say, my cheeks burning hot.

"It doesn't translate well," she says.

"Well I'm fine," I say. "I had it, but thank him for his help anyway."

Lana purses her lips then nods and speaks to Ragnar. He holds up his hands then walks away.

Light-headiness rushes over me watching him leave. His tail shifts side to side. Thick, long, and filling my head with wondering what the rest of him might look like. The distraction is too much.

"Are you okay?" Lana asks, cutting through my daydreams.

"Yeah," I say, exhaling heavily.

"They can do that," she smiles.

"What?" Uhuh, still brilliant.

Lana turns her gaze towards Ragnar's retreating form, then back. My heart thumps hard in my chest as heat floods my cheeks.

"Oh, uh, no, yeah, uhm," I stutter.

Lana doesn't laugh. She hugs me, just like her mom did, then I'm left standing here with only my sense of embarrassment.

The Zmaj are moving so I head over to the group of women standing by the entrance to the valley. It's a nice place, if you like to rough it. Who am I to judge? We live in the wreckage of our ship. The valley walls have caves cut into the stone which lead into a network of rooms. Awnings that used to stand outside some of the entrances where the craftsmen worked are down and packed.

The pirates found us here and while we fought them off and took their transport vehicle, there's no doubt they'll be back. Lana says the Zmaj know them well and that they're slavers. They capture and sell people. That would have happened to Delilah and me if Astarot and Lana hadn't been on the same transport.

Since the pirates know this place exists now, it's only a matter of time before they come back. It was a debate but Astarot and Lana have talked the Zmaj here into moving to their home. A city, they say. I find it hard to believe there's a city on this sandy ball of hell, but we'll see.

The other survivors from her section of the ship are there and more Zmaj.

On our way there we'll stop by my home. The question then is do I go on with them to the new city or stay with my friends? The city sounds nice. She says they have a dome working that keeps the sandstorms out and the wandering monsters too. Buildings, actual honest-to-goodness buildings. I'm a little sick of caves and tilted wreckages.

The Commander taps his staff on the stone and everyone falls silent. He speaks, then we all turn and walk out of the valley. I notice several of the Zmaj glance over their shoulders with what looks like regret. I get how hard it is to lose your home.

We pack like sardines onto the transport along with the supplies.

It's a box like contraption with a ramp on one side. Inside are three sections. The front which has room for two, maybe three people, connected by a small hallway to the center area which has a door that leads to another open area with shelves for supplies. We're packed in so tight that there's no sitting or moving around. I'm squashed up against a wall, my breasts smashed to the point of being uncomfortable. It smells of sweat, dirt, and sand. Somehow, my bad or good luck I'm not sure, Ragnar is standing up against my backside.

The machine hums to life, rising, which causes all of us to jostle. Ragnar's mammoth thigh and knee press into my ass as the vehicle shifts side to side. I think nothing of it at first, but it remains firmly crushed against my backside once the transport's motion has settled. Glancing over my shoulder, my eyes meet his and the analyzing part of my mind clicks, figuring out our positions relative to each other and what part of him is actually thrust against my rear.

My eyes widen, my mouth drops open, and I gasp. Surely it's not...

The transport rocks side to side and again the thickness mashes against the globes of my butt.

I'm certain now, he's aroused.

That massive firmness I mistook for his thigh is his cock! How big is it?

Maybe Zmaj males don't work like human men. Are they aroused all the time? It can't be because of me.

He's still staring though, making my skin grow warm.

The transport bounces with violence and everyone staggers. My knees buckle and I'd fall but there's not enough room to, I'm held up by the press of bodies. It drives Ragnar's immense hard-on deeper into my cheeks. My own lady-boner is raging and if I was alone I wouldn't hesitate to rub one out. In this situation there's nothing I can do.

By the time the transport slows, I can barely think. My clit aches and I'm considering throwing myself onto Ragnar the moment I can turn around. The vehicle drops, settling back to the ground, and everyone in the cargo area sighs with relief. We've been in here for hours, crammed up against each other with just enough room to breathe if you don't inhale too deeply.

Light appears along the side opposite of me as the ramp rumbles to life and lowers. The double red suns strike through the opening like a spear. Dots swirl before my eyes as they struggle to adjust from near blackness to blinding light. I can't see, but someone gasps, then I'm being pushed and pulled along as the crowd rushes out.

"NO!" someone is screaming.

My eyes are watering, still struggling to adjust. Something smells off, gross and disgusting that makes me regret leaving behind the sweat and dirt odor of the transport. My stomach clenches in a violent spasm. The spinning dots clear from my eyes and then the odors make sense. Soot and burnt meat. It can't be….

My home lies before me in ruin, its defensive walls shattered. The refuge we'd built from salvaged material, the workstations, the tables, everything is overturned, destroyed. Debris litters the landscape. Smoke pours out of the wreckage of the ship itself, carrying with it that stench.

Tears flow down my face, my throat clenches tight. They're gone. No one is here. All my friends, gone.

I stumble forward in a daze, full of dread.

There are so many grayish lumps all around, my mind rejects the impossibility of what they are. I can't stand any longer, my knees buckle and I fall. My hands shake as I stare at the horrifying, charred balls. A hot wind blows my streaming tears onto the sand with a soft sizzle. A piece of cloth shifts in the breeze, dislodging a blackened hunk that rolls towards me.

It's cold when I touch it.

"OH!" I scream, falling backwards, then I'm scrambling away.

It can't be, no, this isn't happening.

It's a nightmare.

People are screaming and crying all around as I crawl back into something rigid and unmoving.

I look up into Ragnar's deep blue eyes.

Hand shaking, I point at the lump. "It's a skull," I say, my chest heaving with sobs. "They're all... someone mur-"

I can't say the words. The words will make it real and this can't be.

Ragnar kneels and enfolds me in a protective embrace and I break down.

2

RAGNAR

*L*ooking the burnt wreckage over, it's obvious the Zzlo are responsible.

If there are survivors, they've been captured and are on their way to being slaves.

The curvy, thick one I long to grasp hold of and claim as my treasure is shaking and mewling like a newborn. She's lost everything, that's a feeling I know. Lana has told me Olivia is her name.

She doesn't see me as she blindly stumbles back away from the carnage into my arms. When she gazes up with wide, green eyes, I can't help that my cock jumps to life. I enfold her soft, full body in an embrace but she doesn't let me hold her long before pushing away.

I let her go and she rises and walks off as I watch to make sure she's not going too far from safety.

She doesn't, she simply starts picking up odd debris and looking at things.

Astarot and Lana huddle together with the Commander by the transport so I walk over to see what they're thinking.

"Shit," Lana says, as I approach.

It's easy to see how shaken she is. Her skin is paler than normal and there is moisture in the corners of her eyes; I've seen the other human females do this, it means they're upset. Astarot puts his arm over her shoulders and pulls her to him. Looking over her head he casts a questioning look at me.

"We should go back," I say.

"Back?" he asks.

"Yes, this is dangerous. We can defend the valley. Here, we're exposed with no viable defense. It's more than obvious that the Zzlo have been here. No animal on Tajss would do this."

"The valley is not defensible," he says.

"We can make it so," I argue.

"Don't be a fool," Lana says, whirling to face me.

Anger flashes white hot and the bijass roars to life. The bijass is everything primal and dominating. Trembling with the effort to remain in control, I hiss. Astarot pushes his mate behind him and glares.

"Edicts," he hisses.

I'm still struggling but nod my understanding. Edicts. Edicts are edicts, edicts bring us together. I repeat it to myself until the bijass retreats.

"Yes," I say. "But this is stupid, we need to go back to the valley."

They say nothing, staring at me as if I'm the dumb one. Astarot and I glare at each other until I turn and walk away. My brother, Ryuth, is in chains in the back of the transport. Locked away from the rest of us until we can figure out how to undo what the Zzlo did to him. I don't know how long they've kept him in slavery, long enough to force him to attack his own kind and not recognize his own brother. I can't help him out here in the desert. I need time and room to work with him, time to reach the man buried within the bijass.

The other hunters, Bashir and Melchior, have climbed to the top of a nearby dune. If I can get them to agree then maybe together we can convince the Commander. They turn as I approach, lifting their wings in silent greeting. I return the gesture as I join them on top of the dune.

"Anything?" I ask.

"Tracks lead off that way," Bashir says, pointing off towards the setting suns.

"Burn them," Melchior hisses.

"I know," I say, putting a hand on his back.

"They have to have a way to get the humans off world, there's nowhere here they can sell them," Bashir says.

"I agree," I say. "They're gone."

"We're short of females still," Melchior says, always the practical one.

"Yes, we are," I say.

"Should we try to rescue them?" Bashir asks.

"No. They're gone, probably already off world. How would we get to them?" I reply.

Bashir nods while Melchior's tail shifts back and forth and his wings rustle in agitation.

"We're too exposed, this is bad," Melchior says.

"I agree," I say, suppressing my smile.

My hunters, there is a bond between the three of us that runs deep. We have worked together for years and I know them as they know me. The survival of the Tribe has been on us since the Devastation. Kalessin pulled us together but none knew how to survive in the new world. We learned, the three of us forged a bond in the fires of the hunt. Nothing could form a deeper connection than knowing your life depends on the Zmaj next to you.

The three of us stare out over the empty, rolling red dunes watching the suns drop to the horizon. Something crashes behind us, drawing our attention. Turning, Olivia is grabbing debris off the ground and throwing it.

"What is that female doing?" Bashir asks.

"I do not know," I say, leaving them behind as I go to find out.

Ducking a flying sheet of metal as I approach, I hold up my hands in front of me trying to placate the upset female. Water streams down her face, she's yelling. It might be words, I don't know, just that they are screeching sounds coming out of her as she continues to grab pieces and throw them.

She doesn't stop. Maybe this is a ritual for the females? I don't understand but I can help her. She bends down and grabs a charred hunk of metal, lifting it over her head with an effort. I step closer and take it from her. She looks up at me, wide-eyed, and screams. I throw the mass as far as I can out into the desert, gaining a much greater distance than the objects she's thrown previously.

She stares at me, mouth open, shaking. It might be helping so I grab the next closest thing off the ground and throw it too. It's a flat sheet that catches the wind well, causing it to sore farther still. Olivia shakes her head side to side, eyes still wide. Her mouth snaps shut, and she quits screaming. Good, it is helping!

Moving quickly, I grab up piece after piece and throw them for her. She says something I don't understand but I'm sure she must be thanking me. When I turn back towards her, Lana is running up. Good, she can translate. I want Olivia to understand this isn't a problem for me and that I'm happy to have been of help to her.

"Ragnar what are you doing?" Lana asks, her voice cracking as she runs up.

"I'm helping," I answer, wondering how it cannot be obvious.

Lana talks to Olivia. They speak fast in their own tongue, words too harsh, filled with hard sounds I don't understand. Olivia balls her fists then throws her hands up in the air. She screams something at Lana then points at me. What has Lana done?

"Uh, Ragnar, that's not helping."

"What do you mean? She was throwing things. I am helping her with this."

Lana stares, her mouth open, her eyes blinking fast, then shakes her head.

"Uhm," she says.

I stare, waiting for her to explain how I am not being helpful.

Olivia speaks, rapid fire, then turns and walks away with moisture streaming down her face.

"What is she saying?" I ask, struggling to keep the bijass under control. Edicts, I remind myself.

"Look," Lana says, placing a hand on my arm. "It's just… different. She's upset, she's lost her friends. Maybe you should just give her some space."

"Space?" I ask, still confused. I motion around myself with my arm. "There is nothing but space here. She can have all she likes of it, I do not own this space. If she wants it, I will take it for her."

Lana smiles rubbing my arm with her hand.

"I know you would," she says, chuckling.

"Why are you laughing?" I ask, black fog roiling in my mind, making it harder to stay in control.

"Nothing," she says. "Sorry, just, let her walk around, okay?"

Gritting my teeth together I nod my agreement. It is not as if I have a choice. I don't understand these females, the things they do make no sense. Still, the dragon inside covets the ample-bodied female. It demands I claim Olivia as my treasure, nothing less will do. I will have her, I will bury my hard cock in her softness.

"Fine," I snap, turning and walking away before the dark clouds claim me.

None of this makes sense. We should be in the valley. We've survived there and there's no reason we can't continue to survive there. The Zzlo might try to take us but we would defeat them again. Out here, we're exposed.

Glancing over my shoulder, Olivia is talking with Lana. Lana holds out her arms and Olivia steps into them, laying her head on Lana's shoulder. It should be my shoulder her head rests on. Rage flares up like a roaring furnace, swallowing me whole. I've turned and am walking back towards them before I know it.

Edicts! Edicts bring us together.

My fading conscience screams, chanting the mantra, pushing the rage of the bijass back, reclaiming control. Stopping in my tracks, I stare at them only a moment before turning around. Bashir and Melchior watch me from the top of the dune, silent in their understanding. No words needed between us.

"We need to turn around," I snap, as I reach them. "Come with me."

They fall in silently as I lead the way back down the dune towards the transport. The Commander, Visidion, is still talking with Astarot. Lana is approaching at the same time my hunters and I are.

"We should get moving," Astarot says.

"I agree," Visidion replies.

"I'll gather them up," Lana says. "It's obvious the pirates are close, we should get out of here quickly."

"Hold," I say and everyone turns towards me.

"What is it?" Astarot asks.

"This is a terrible idea, we need to go back to the valley," I say.

Lana and Astarot look at each other but I don't care what their opinions are, my attention locks with Visidion.

"Ragnar, I've made the choice," he says, leaning heavy on his staff.

"Choices can change. We're exposed, the Zzlo have been here. What defense can we mount out here?"

"You know damn we can't defend the valley!" Lana says, stepping forward.

"No, I don't. All I know is that you two," I point at her and Astarot, "say a lot of words. Pretty words. There's a city, there's others, we can all be together. Your words mean nothing. You've upended everything!"

The bijass rises, vying for control. I struggle, forced to split my attention between them and it.

"Don't be a fool," Lana snaps.

White-hot rage. My hands ball into fists so tight my claws bite into the palms of my hands. My wings spread of their own accord and my skin is burning. No one calls me a fool. I've earned my right as leader of the hunt.

"Stand down, female," I hiss.

Astarot steps between us, his tail is slashing left and right, his wings are spreading. I step, ready to take him on. His female is crossing the line.

"Ragnar, no," Visidion says.

"No what?" I yell, whirling to him. "Why are you listening to these outsiders? How do you know they didn't bring the Zzlo? They could be working with them!"

"You've got to be kidding me!" Lana yells.

"Ragnar, be serious," Astarot says.

"No, I'm done. We'll not follow your guidance any longer. We can defend the valley. It's safer than we are out here," I say, making a slashing motion with my hand to cut him off.

"Ragnar, do not do this," Visidion says. "Have faith."

"I do, in my men," I hiss. "Not these outsiders."

"You're insane," Lana says from behind Astarot.

The rage burns hot and the edicts aren't helping. Trembling, I take a step towards her.

Astarot and I square off as I drop to a crouch, ready to attack. He leans forward with his fists raised.

"Enough!" Visidion demands.

All the others have stopped to watch the commotion but I don't take my eyes off of Astarot, waiting for Visidion to speak.

"We cannot fight amongst ourselves. We will continue to the City," he says.

"No," I say, stomping my foot to the sandy ground. Straightening, I turn and look at the gathered crowd. "The hunters and I are going home, where we belong," I say, raising my voice. "Any who wish may join us."

Everyone mutters, looking at each other. Pushing my way through them, I find Bashir and Melchior waiting on the far side. The three of us head out into the desert on our own.

If anyone wants to come, let them follow.

3

OLIVIA

The stupid desert stretches out as far as I can see. The reddish sand sparkles under the double suns.

They're gone. All of them, gone. Cold tendrils wind their way from my core to my limbs. The tears have stopped, at last, but my eyes and face still feel puffy and sore.

I should have been here.

A hot wind blows, shifting the sands. Each grain moves in slow motion, crawling along, swirling and dancing.

They're gone, all my friends, gone.

It pounds in my head over and over. Gone, gone, gone.

If I'd been here... what? I'd have done what? Nothing, except get captured or killed too.

Shaking my head at my foolishness I kneel and take two handfuls of sand then watch as it streams between my fingers. Like sands through an hourglass... these are the days of our lives. I snort at my stupidity. My life maybe but theirs are over.

The ones who dies are probably the lucky ones, the rest will be sold into slavery. Just when I think this world has gotten as absolutely shitty as it possibly could, it finds a new way to be even shittier.

"Damn it!" Lana yells, pulling my attention out of the black morass of my thoughts.

Rising, I turn and realize for the first time how far from the group I've wandered. Lana is gesturing wildly, Astarot and Visidion stand next to her. Ragnar is walking away from the group and the other two hunters are with him. It doesn't take any special insight to see what's going on. Ragnar hasn't wanted to make this trip from the beginning. It was his opinion we should stay at the Valley and mount a defense against the pirates.

Ragnar and the hunters have gone quite a ways into the desert already. Lana and the two Zmaj with her argue with each other while Ragnar and his group increase their distance. I should help.

What can I do? Nothing. I can do nothing.

No, that's stupid. Do I give in to despair? Is that the girl my momma raised? Give up because things have gotten hard?

It'd be easier. A deep lethargic urge to just not move pulls me down, roots me in place. So easy to just stay right here, wallowing in the loss of everyone.

Again.

That's the worst part, we lost everything when the ship crashed. Friends, family, all my family gone. Co-workers, life as we knew it, gone. You think you know where your life is going then pirates attack and rip those expectations away. The smoke and screams as my world turned upside down then sped towards this shit-snack of a planet.

This is survival. Pure and simple. All complexities get washed away when it takes all you've got to make sure you'll be alive in the next moment, the next hour. When not seeing the suns rise the next day becomes a very real possibility, it strips you down to the core of yourself.

If I will continue to survive, I can't let myself fall into the dark well of hopelessness that wants to claim me. It's there, I can't deny it, all those feelings are real but I have to get in motion. Start somewhere, put one foot in front of the other.

Slow exhale as I walk. Maybe I can help. Doing what I have no idea, but I have to try. It's an act of will to force myself to keep moving. Each step though becomes easier. The black despair is there, waiting, pulling me down with clinging fingers that don't want to let go but I can't give in.

Lana says something and then points at the fading forms of Ragnar and the hunters.

Following her finger I see that a handful of the other Zmaj have joined them.

Visidion replies then Astarot says something. Damn I wish I knew their language. Astarot stares at their retreating backs, his tail shifts side to side with nervous agitation.

"Maybe I can help?" I say, walking up.

"How?" Lana asks.

"Uh, I don't know," I say, blushing as self-consciousness rushes over me.

The black despair returns like a tidal wave, the current of it pulling me down. Tears swell as I struggle to breathe. My chest constricts, my stomach knots with churning acid and I'm sure I will pass out. The faces of my friends and my family swim before my eyes.

No.

I'm not going to give in. I'm alive, I'm here. I can help, damn it I can do this! Closing my eyes tight to hold back my tears, I take a deep breath. Something touches my arm, when I open my eyes Lana is there, her grip firm on my arm. We stare into each other's eyes and in her I find strength. I lost a lot, but it's not over and I'm not done.

"Ragnar, I can talk to him," I say.

The two Zmaj stare at us, causing me a flash of discomfort but that's just as ridiculous as letting my emotions overwhelm me. There are over a dozen Zmaj and a small handful of women milling around. What are we going to do? Sit here and wait for the pirates to take us too?

Lana translates to Astarot and Visidion. They three of them go back and forth. Shifting my weight from foot to foot, I wait for them to reach an agreement. I stare across the desert at Ragnar's retreating form. He stops and looks back and I know, deep in my heart, he's looking at me. The distance is too great for me to see him as more than an indistinct blob but I'm certain.

"Okay," Lana says.

"Huh?" I ask, my attention jerking back.

"Okay," she says. "No one has a better idea. We're counting on you. We need them."

"Yeah, okay," I say, butterflies dancing a minuet in my stomach.

No pressure Olivia, they're just all counting on you.

"Everybody!" Lana yells, then says what I assume is the same thing in Zmaj. "Please load on the transport."

"Why?" Delilah asks. "What the hell's the point?"

"Where are they going?" Penelope asks, pointing at the dim figures on the horizon.

"We're going to handle that," Lana says. "Let's get moving."

The Zmaj look at Visidion and the human women look at each other but no one jumps into motion. Lana's face flushes pink then deep red. She purses her lips and balls her hands into fists.

"Hey," I say, no idea what I'm doing. "I know. This is... awful. Trust me, I feel it too. What are we going to do though? Stand here? Wait for the pirates to come take us? Look, we don't have many options. The best thing I can see right now is for us to join up with the other survivors. Maybe, and I know this is a long shot, but maybe we can help our friends. If we stay here that ain't happening."

Certainty fills me as I speak. I hadn't thought out what I would say before I said it. The words spilled out of my mouth almost like they were coming from someone else, but the moment I said them they were true. True for me at least. Maybe we can save them. At least in moving forward there's hope.

The women mutter and nod then they move onto the transport. Visidion says something, then Lana replies in the Zmaj language, but the Zmaj men are already following the women onto the transport. It takes time for us to all get on. Even with Ragnar and his followers gone we're packed tight.

The transport rumbles then lifts and we're in motion. Since it's designed for transporting slaves, there is no comfort. No windows, no air, just a dark box and the press of bodies against each other. I miss Ragnar being here.

Why did he leave me?

Self-doubt rears its ugly head again.

I'm being ridiculous. The least I can do is help. The transport bumps and rumbles causing us all to shift.

"Oh!" someone cries out as it lunges violently again.

The sound of metal on metal screeches through the small space, then the transport jerks and I'm smashed against the wall. The floor shifts and I slam side to side. A scream slips out then the world flips.

I can't tell up from down.

My head cracks against something, stars swim in my vision.

I'm being crushed. Can't breathe.

Moaning, screams, tears, need air.

The blackness is as crushing as the bodies pressed against me.

"Anyone hurt?" someone asks.

"Yes," someone else cries.

I try to respond but I can't get enough air. Gasping, trying to inhale, my chest is being crushed. It's impossible. Awareness is fading, pulling me down.

Something is pounding, louder than the moans. Bodies shift and a quick breath of air fills my lungs bringing sweet relief. Another shift and the crushing weight returns. Someone is crying, I'm sure it's not me, I don't have enough air for tears.

Light! Bright, searing white, it burns into my eyes.

"OLIVIA!"

4

RAGNAR

*E*verything has gone wrong. It's Astarot's fault. Everything was fine until he showed up.

"We're at least three days out," Bashir says.

"I know," I respond.

"They're following," Melchior adds.

Stopping, I turn and look. The cloud of dust the transport raises in its passing is heading towards us. Closing my protective lids, I can see the transport itself racing ahead of the streaming cloud.

"What do you want to do?" Bashir asks.

"What I want is to go home," I say.

My chest constricts, making my hearts work harder. Do my friends see what I won't say? What I want? The way she calls to me? The distance doesn't matter, I can sense her approach.

"It'd be easier with them," Melchior says. "Long walk otherwise."

I glare at Melchior until his tail drops to the ground and he bows his head.

"Let them come," I say. "I'll handle it when they arrive."

Without further comment I turn and resume walking. It's foolish, feeling this way. I don't know how she feels but every time I'm near her desire consumes me. My body aches, my cocks become so hard it hurts. Nothing has ever made me feel the way she does.

I can't tell the others, even if I know they'd understand. I've seen them eying females, too.

The ground trembles and all of us stop. Bashir raises his fist then holds up one finger at a time reaching a count of five. Damn it, its close. The sand shifts as the trembling increases. Staring ahead, the line of shifting sand comes right at us. Moving in slow motion, each hunter takes a spear off his back, preparing.

Arawn and Errol, the craftsmen who followed, hold still too. They know, we all know. Tajss is full of dangers but nothing is more dangerous that a zemlja. The giant dragon worm that burrows beneath the surface hunts by vibrations. Depending on its age and size it could be a challenge or a death sentence, even for the five of us.

The trembling increases, the sands shifting faster. My breath catches in my throat and I grip my spear tighter. Any moment. It will either pass us by or the ground will erupt and we'll be fighting for survival.

Hot wind blows across my face as we wait, hoping. None of us wants to fight a zemlja. The shifting sand slows, the trembling fades, and it's gone past.

Letting out the breath I'd been holding, I look over at Bashir. He's looking past me then his eyes widen and his mouth opens.

I know, before I turn, I know.

"No!" I yell, whirling.

The transport flies up into the air, tumbling over itself. It slams into the ground then bounces up into the air again. My hearts stop. Air won't come into my lungs. My stomach is a tight knot of fear. Olivia!

My feet slam into the ground as I run. Each step I jump, leaping into the air and spread my wings to glide further, gaining speed.

I don't wait for my hunters. There's no time. She's on that transport. I have to reach her.

Ahead, the ground explodes and the giant dragon-worm rises into the sky. It's massive, an ancient. Quite possibly thousands of years old to be so large.

It waves back and forth then slams the ground, searching for prey. The transport tumbles over again and the loud crash draws its attention. Its maw opens and it tries to bite. A loud screech echoes across the sands as its teeth slide across the metal of the transport.

"NO!" I scream, waving my spear, trying to distract the monster from my treasure.

I'm hit from behind, tumbling to the ground and rolling over, struggling to break free.

Coming to a stop Melchior is on top of me.

"Get off!" I scream, but he puts a hand over my mouth, forcing my jaw closed.

I swing, punching him in the side of the head. Kicking with my legs and swinging my tail to one side I force him to roll with me to keep his grip. On top I stand and step back. His tail takes me in the legs, sweeping them out from under me. As I fall to the ground, Bashir lands on top, then he and Melchior pin me from either side.

"Let me go!" I scream.

"Ragnar, stop," Bashir says.

"I have to save her," I scream, fighting with all I have.

Almost, I'm almost free. She needs me.

"Wait, she's fine," Bashir says.

Rage fills me and with it comes the gray fog of the bijass.

She's mine, nothing will threaten her, nothing will harm her. Not while I draw breath.

They force me to my feet, turning so I can see the transport. The zemlja tries to bite it again, the scraping screech of its teeth echos across the dunes. The transport rocks back and forth then the zemlja lowers down beneath the surface.

The ground trembles, shifting as it digs its way deeper. The hunters hold onto me until the trembling ground stops, leaving silence in its wake. Jerking my arms free, I run for the transport. My long strides and my ability to glide with my wings eats up the ground between me and my goal.

The transport lies on its side, long scrapes gouged into the metal where the zemlja tried to eat it. Leaping, I land on top of the transport in a crouch. It came to a stop with the door facing up. The metal is bent and twisted just enough that I can get a grip on the edge. Inside there are muffled cries for help.

Adrenaline rushes through my body. A euphoric feeling fills me and along with it comes the bijass, stronger than ever. Edicts, I remind myself, holding a line against my primal desire. Sliding my fingertips into the crack, I grip the metal and then pull. Straining, I put all I have into it. A scraping sound rewards my effort but the metal barely budges.

A thump sounds as Melchior lands next to me followed by Bashir. They move in and take what grip they can find. The three of us pull, the metal resists us, but I will beat it. Olivia is in there. Visions of her lying hurt and in pain fill my mind and I hiss with anger, pulling harder.

The metal moves but I lose my grip, stumbling backwards. Spreading my wings I come to a stop on the edge of the transport. Bashir and Melchior reach out, grabbing for me, but I'm able to keep myself from going over the edge. Rage roars in my blood. Nothing will stand between her and

I, nothing! Stomping back into place I grab the metal and pull with renewed vigor.

My hunters redouble their efforts. The cold steel bends, slow, an inch at a time. A black hole forms as the steel peels back, creating an opening into the transport.

"OLIVIA!" I yell, the hard sounds strange on my tongue. I've never said her name aloud before.

People cry out, some in pain, some in relief. We pull until there's an opening large enough for a Zmaj to pass through. Looking down into the pale, dirty faces staring into the light, I search for her. When I don't see Olivia the rage rises but no, reason. The edicts, I cannot give in to my primal side.

"Get them out of there," I order, my voice tight as I struggle to contain it.

Bashir drops to the ground, Melchior moves to one side, and I lay flat, reaching in to the dark hole and grabbing the first hand I can. Pulling, another female's dirty face rises into the light. There is a cut on her head and blood is running down her face. She blinks rapidly, saying strange words that make no sense. She is not Olivia so I pass her to Melchior who lowers her to Bashir.

We work as quickly as we can but it takes too long. Each hand I grab, I expect to see Olivia rising from the dark but each time it's someone else. Cursing, I pull them out faster. The males inside are pushing the females out from below, helping them up first, speeding up the process.

"Olivia!" I cry out in overwhelming frustration.

"Ragnar!"

Her voice is sweet water after a long hunt.

She is alive.

A hand grasps mine and I grip, then pull and Olivia's head rises from the dark hole. A joy such as I've never felt fills me. There are cuts on her cheeks and one of her eyes is swelling and turning a dark purple, but she is alive. I pull her straight up, rising with her and taking her in my arms.

She wraps hers around my waist and lays her head against my chest. She talks but words make no difference. She is alive. Nothing else matters. Resting my chin on her head I hold her tight to my body. My cock is raging hard and part of me wants to take her here and now, let all see my claim of this female.

That is the bijass and I know it, so I push back. Letting her go, our fingers trail across each other as Melchior takes her then lowers her to Bashir. I pull the other Zmaj out of the transport until Drosdan is the only one left. He is bigger than any of us, so large he can climb out without my help. He is standing in the light looking up then shakes his head, holding up a hand.

"A moment," he says, then disappears into the dark.

While waiting for him to return, metal scrapes on metal, a clinking noise that moves closer to the sounds of a struggle. A wordless cry filled with anger comes out of the hole then Drosdan appears in the light. My brother is slung over his shoulder, struggling against the chains we bound him with.

When the Zzlo attacked the Valley, my brother was with them, at least his body was. He has regressed into the bijass so deeply that he's little more than a primal animal. I can only imagine what they've done to make him this way. Wild, running on instinct. He fought with the fury of a cornered animal. We captured him when we beat the Zzlo and sent them into retreat but I've not had time to help him.

I'm certain, given time, I can bring him back from the dark fog that covers his mind. He, the brother I love, is still in there behind the rage of the bijass. I will reach him.

Drosdan lifts Ryuth with difficulty. Drosdan is big and muscular, but lifting a full grown, bound and struggling Zmaj over your head is no easy task.

I get a grip on the chains that bind Ryuth and pull. He hisses when he sees me, his eyes are red as are the edges of his scales. Rage has its claws deep. An empty ache pulses in my chest as I lower my brother down to Bashir. By the time I do, Drosdan has pulled himself out of the transport. Our gazes meet and he nods. We don't need to speak, he knows I appreciate his act.

Leaping off the transport, I glide to a landing next to Visidion, the Elders, and Astarot. They're debating our next move. Of course they are, too much talk. That's the problem with all of them. They talk when there is no choice but to act. Shaking my head as I listen, a cold certainty forms in my gut.

I rarely speak at Council, but now I must. "Enough," I say, making a slicing motion with my hand.

"You have something to add?" Visidion asks.

"Yes," I say, looking into the eyes of each male standing close. "This talking is accomplishing nothing. The wounded need tending. We have no transport and no shelter. It's time to gather supplies, tend the wounded, and move."

"Agreed," Astarot says.

Lana walks up beside him, placing her arm around his waist and he puts an arm over her shoulders. Cold, hard jealousy stabs into my heart like a knife. A quick glance and I spot Olivia sitting in the shade of the transport, another female tending to her wounds.

"Ragnar, can you and the hunters form something to carry our supplies?" Visidion asks.

"Yes," I say.

The females have grouped together in the shade of the transport. There is moisture dripping off of them, inefficient and wasteful. None of them look well. They're not adjusted to the heat of Tajss and it's obvious they won't hold up for long.

My choice becomes clear.

"There is epis in your City?" I ask Astarot.

"Yes," he says.

I make my decision. "Bashir, Melchior, get with Arawn and make a travois to carry the supplies. Padraig will pull the most weight without it slowing him. We need to move, go."

They jump to work at my command. Walking after them, a touch slows me. I look down at the small, red tinged hand, then follow it up to meet Lana's eyes.

"The City?" she asks.

I nod and pull away. The wreck of the transport made my choice. I have to get Olivia to shelter and epis. There is no other choice.

Glancing over my shoulder, my hearts skip a beat as she pushes herself off the transport to her feet. She looks over at me and smiles, tentative, unsure, before joining the line that is forming to haul what supplies we can carry.

The suns are hanging low on the horizon by the time we finish. Depending on Lana to translate orders to the females isn't helping speed things up. Lana asks too many questions. My men listen, they do what they're ordered without all the need for asking why.

At last we're ready to move out. Two long sticks with leathers woven between them form a traveling travois. Arawn rigged straps that loop over Padraig's shoulders. Even with dividing the supplies amongst the Zmaj, we're leaving behind a lot but there isn't any other option. Survival will be hard but with luck we'll make it.

"I'm not an animal," Padraig grouses as I walk by.

"I know," I say, stopping to face him.

He glowers. He's tall enough it cranes my neck to look at him. He rolls his shoulders, shakes his head, then huffs.

"Fine," he agrees.

"Move out!" I call.

Bashir takes the lead as instructed. Melchior wanders far

off to the left, just keeping our line in sight. They're my eyes and ears, skilled hunters who know the signs of danger giving us the best chance of being prepared for what might come.

The Zmaj men form a loose, protective circle around the females but it doesn't last long. The humans can't move well on the sand. Lana has her strange looking shoes that allow her to move easier, but the rest sink in with every step, struggling for each forward motion. We're traveling at less than a third of the speed I estimated.

I don't have to say a word. The males move in and help the females which speeds things up but is still slower than I want. We can't carry them and the supplies. The best we can do is offer them some help, pulling them out when they sink in too deep to move on their own.

Olivia is having the hardest time. Her luscious curves and full chest cause her to sink deep. Every step is torture on her face. Staying by her side, the line of the others draws further and further ahead. She talks, often, and I wish I knew what she was saying.

I will not leave her side. Olivia's determination is stunning. She's panting, moisture drips off her bright red face, her equally bright red hair is plastered to her head. Yet she still pushes forward.

Stopping, she drinks water from her container, then offers it. Holding up my hand I decline. Water will be our most precious resource on this journey and she needs it far more than I do.

The suns are low on the horizon and dropping fast. Shadows encroach, making it difficult to see the line of the others ahead. They'll be setting up camp soon, we'll catch up then. Olivia looks ahead, shields her eyes, takes several deep breaths then leans in and resumes walking.

As we climb a dune, circumventing a large rock formation, twinkling fire lights dot the landscape ahead. Her arms tremble and she's moving slower, but she's still pushing forward. We're close enough now, I can help more. Shifting the pack on my back I put an arm around her. She looks up at me with wide-eyes and an open mouth, pushing me away but I don't let her stop me.

Swinging my other arm under her waist I sweep her off her feet and into my arms. Spreading my wings I bound across the desert to camp. I wish I could have carried her like this entire way but even my strength has its limits. She wraps her arms around my neck, holding herself close. A soft, tingling sensation crawls across my scales. It's almost enough to make me shiver.

As we enter the camp, the smell of cooking bivo reaches my nostrils and brings a smile. We didn't bring shelters, but I made sure there are blankets for the females. They've set them up in concentric circles around small fires. Olivia pushes against my chest, speaking fast, making me wish yet again that I could understand what she's saying. She struggles so I put her down.

She straightens her clothes while making quick glances around. Her skin is flushed pink even though the suns have dropped below the horizon. I don't understand why she would still be this color. Reaching to touch her face she pulls back.

Anger flashes white hot. I don't understand why she's acting this way.

Edicts, the edicts bring us together.

Closing my eyes, I recite them. I'd never hurt her, no matter how much of me the bijass might claim, but it still reacts to the stabbing pain in my hearts when she withdraws.

She frowns, touches my face, then shakes her head. If only we could speak.

Pointing, I lead the way through the fires towards the one

Bashir and Melchior have set up, knowing they will have made a space for me. Bashir grabs one rod holding meat over the fire and pulls several chunks off it, lying them on a piece of oiled cloth. He holds it out as I take my seat.

Olivia sits down next to me and I offer her some. She takes a piece, handling it delicately as she blows on it to cool it. While we eat, Bashir updates me on our progress. We made more headway than I expected after seeing the speed the females could manage, which is good. Olivia chats with the other two women sitting at our circle. She seems happy and they do too. I hope, with some luck, that our journey will remain good for them.

"Did you hear that?" Melchior asks, cocking his head to one side and reaching for the spear at his side.

It's the only warning we have before loud screeches cut through the night. The females scream as one rising, warbling voice that echoes through the night.

5

OLIVIA

*R*agnar carried me the last little bit to the camp and it was so damn romantic and embarrassing at the same time.

Like admitting I couldn't do it on my own, but also the kindest thing anyone has ever done for me.

Now we're having dinner and I chat with Astrid and Delilah. The two Zmaj that are always close to Ragnar, I can't keep their names straight, share our fire.

"This sucks," Astrid sighs, wiping grease from her fingers on her pants.

"What does?" I ask.

"All of it."

"Yeah."

"What the hell are we doing? What's next?" she asks. "We get something of a life put together, then I'm kidnapped by these alien dragon men. That all works out okay and I think things will be alright, then we find out that the stupid space pirates have taken all our friends?"

She shakes her head, hunching her shoulders over.

"It's a total shit show," Delilah pipes in.

One of the hunters tilts his head and says something to Ragnar. Melchior, I think his name is, maybe? Or is that the other one?

All three Zmaj grab their spears and leap to their feet. The girls and I look at each other. I don't hear anything but it's obvious they do. Jumping to my feet, I look around trying to spot anything.

A moment later something dives out of the sky making a screeching sound that sends cold chills racing up and down my spine. My guts lock tight as I drop to the sand, throwing my arms up to protect my head.

Ragnar steps backwards, almost trampling me.

Realizing this is a terrible and stupid position, I stand back up. Every nerve of my body screams that I should curl into a ball and pray for it to pass. My instincts suck.

Ragnar whirls his spear around, driving it up into the air and then spins it the other way. He moves with a stunning, beautiful fluidity and skill. Like watching a dancer. My core tightens. The way his muscles flex is an impressive display of strength that makes me clench my thighs.

They Zmaj warriors are effective, driving back the diving balls of teeth and death.

Penelope screams from behind a Zmaj at the fire next to us. Three of the creatures are attacking him. In a display of his own skill he blocks two, driving them back, but the third slips past.

It's almost to my friend. Ragnar leaps, his wings spreading wide, the spear tip glinting in the moonlight as he whirls it into position. He lands and drives it into the body of the beast just before it reaches Penelope.

He spins his spear off to one side then flicks it, sending a dead monster flying. I get my first good look at our attackers as it leaves his spear. It looks like a furry body with wide, leathery wings, rows of sharp teeth and talons that could tear flesh.

It's horrifying, filling me with cold dread knowing more of these flying balls of death are still attacking us.

Ragnar and the Zmaj continue their defensive dance, protecting us. His spear flashes, muscles flex, and I watch in utter fascination.

My body responds to his controlled power, my nipples are so hard the cloth of my shirt scrapes against them sending violent, jolting thrills through me.

The monsters apparently give up, the screeching and faint leathery sounds recede.

Ragnar spins on his heel, stopping to face me. He leaps into the air, his wings spread, then descends to land before me. Beautiful.

He touches my face, looks up and down my body. It takes only a moment to realize he's inspecting me for wounds.

"I'm fine," I say, but he doesn't comprehend.

"Is anyone hurt?" Lana yells.

Responses come back from around the encampment while Ragnar finishes his inspection. His attention does nothing to ease the tension between my thighs, in fact it makes it worse. A pulse-pounding, clit-throbbing need threatens all my sense of propriety.

When he straightens to his full height I touch his cheek. His scales are cool and smooth under my fingertips. I wish, with everything I am, that we could talk.

One of his hands is on my shoulder, the other on my waist. The world fades away until there is only the two of us. Distant sounds become little more than a buzz. My heart pounds in my chest as I rise onto my toes, leaning into Ragnar.

"Are you okay?" Lana asks, cutting right into my moment.

Falling back onto my heels as my attention jerks away

from Ragnar, I bite my lower lip. Tears well in my eye at the sudden pain. Lana grabs me by my shoulders spinning me to face her. Before I can say a word, she's running her hands my arms, gripping me tight.

"I'm fine!" I say, my voice cracking and much louder than it should be.

Lana stops, looking up from the hunched position she was inspecting me from, her surprise obvious. She straightens as my cheeks burn hot. I can't meet her eyes. A crawling desire to find a rock to hide under almost over-whelms me.

"Good," Lana says, looking between Ragnar and me.

Great, just great. She purses her lips and looks like she's going to say something more then shakes her head.

"Is anyone else hurt?" I ask, desperate to get her attention on something else, anything else.

"No," she says. "Seems we came through this okay."

She says something to Ragnar and the sharp, cold steel of jealousy drives into my heart as he answers. What is she saying to him? I want so badly to be able to talk to him, to listen to his voice and know what he's saying. They exchange more words then she snorts and shakes her head. My hands ball into fists as jealousy turns to anger. Is she flirting with him?

Being jealous right now is just stupid. Insecurity is a weakness, one I don't have time for.

Lana smiles at Ragnar then turns back. "I'm glad you're okay, we should all get some sleep," she says. "Tomorrow will be a long day."

"Sure," I say.

Delilah and Astrid are straightening out their blankets and getting ready to lie down so I do the same on my side of the small fire. It's died down to burning embers by the time I get everything straight and lie down. It's nighttime and the sun is down but it's still too hot. This planet sucks.

I sigh, then Ragnar is pressing up against me. His body gives off an easy coolness that pulls me in. He's so much bigger than I. I'm enshrouded, comforted in his safety. I know he won't let anything bad happen.

He touches my hip and I stiffen. Desire blooms fresh at his touch but we're not alone. Discomfort wars with need. How am I supposed to sleep with him so close? As he presses his body against mine, his cock digs into my back. He must be huge!

How am I supposed to sleep now? He's so close, so big, so there, filling my thoughts. I can't relax, pulse pounding need roars through my body, a fire demanding my attention. No, not here and not now.

His hand drifts across my hip, sliding, and damn it if my body doesn't betray me with its desires. I bite my lip as his hand slips under the hem of my pants moving across my folds. One large finger presses hard against my clit, causing me to shudder. A yelp catches in my throat as I'm soaked by my desire.

I can't do this, not here. Grabbing his hand I pull up. He doesn't resist as I push his hand away and place it back on my hip. He lets it rest there, not trying anything else. Slowly my heart returns to a normal pace but by the time it does, his breathing is slow and even against my back.

Great, at least one of us is getting sleep. Lying here, engulfed in his body, the exotic scent of him keeps me awake. At some point I finally drift off to sleep.

SOMEONE IS PUSHING ME. I JERK AWAKE, AWARENESS CRASHING in as adrenaline pumps into my body. Looking around, I'm lost, and it takes a moment to get my bearings. Ragnar is crouched close by, waiting patiently.

Blinking, I stand up and stretch. Sore muscles scream their protest at being forced to move. Sleeping on the ground sucks.

The suns haven't yet broke the horizon but there's enough light to see by, so it's close to dawn. Ragnar holds his hand out with a few chunks of meat. I take two, thank him though it does no good, and pop the cold, chewy meal in my mouth.

It doesn't take long before we're on the move again.

We start out the walk in a group but before the suns have cleared the horizon, the group has become a line and I'm at the back. Again.

Lana has the shoes she designed for moving across the sand and that's great, for her. The rest of us fight for every step in the loose sand. I have to pull my foot out and up then sink down and it's tiring, wearing me down and working muscles I never use.

Once more Ragnar stays close by and helps when I'm having a particularly hard time. The pulling sand is bad enough but it's also all rolling dunes. It seems like I'm always going uphill. Seriously, is there never a slope down? Wiping sweat away from my eyes I pull my water bottle and take a small sip.

I'm trying to be conservative with my water because I don't know when we'll find more. My throat is so dry and parched it hurts to breathe. My body cries out to down the bottle then find more but I can't give in. My head is hurting and I know it will grow until it's a blinding pain.

Resuming my walk I realize how much everything hurts. The suns are high overhead, beating down with relentless energy as they bake the sand and me. Walking through an oven couldn't be much more unpleasant than this.

Ragnar takes my arm and lifts, helping me pull my feet

free and forward.

It's so much easier for him! He's so big you'd think it would be terrible for him but he spreads his wings and glides across the top of the sand like it's nothing. He's a testament to evolutionary theory, perfectly adapted to his environment.

Cresting another dune, I shield my eyes to see how far behind I've fallen. Ragnar stops too. There's a large rock outcropping not very far ahead which casts a long shadow across the sand. That will be nice to walk in when we reach it. The rest of the group is already there. Damn I'm so far behind! Sighing I straighten, adjust my pack, then look further ahead.

"What the hell is that?" I ask pointing into the distance.

It looks like a red-brown wall cutting across the horizon for as far as the eye can see.

Ragnar was watching me but when I point, he turns and looks. He yells, something, I wish to hell I knew what, then he bursts into motion. I'm swept off my feet and into his arms and we're bounding across the desert towards the large rocks. Wrapping my arms around his neck, I hang on for dear life, literally.

He's moving so fast I'm bouncing in his arms like a rag doll. My heart is pounding but there's still a cold ball of ice in the pit of my stomach. I'm jostled hard and bite my tongue, crying out in pain.

Ragnar looks down with concern in his eyes but he doesn't slow.

Well maybe it wasn't concern? What does concern look like on an alien dragon-man's face anyway? Blinking away tears, I strain to look over my shoulder and see the dark wall. It's coming closer, a lot closer, and when I look back ahead we're not gaining very fast on the others. We won't catch up before that wall reaches us.

"Shit," I say, as the sand at my feet stirs in the breeze.

6

RAGNAR

*T*he wind gusts so hard it pushes me to the side. Bits of sand and grit rip across my skin like glass. It tears at my scales and blinding dirt gets in my eyes. I close my protective lids, regaining my vision. Olivia clings tight, both her arms around my neck.

Another gust of wind hits, this time so hard it spins us in a circle. The sand comes with the wind and then the gusts are coming faster and faster. It's whistling across the land, grinding with shredding force. The storm limits my vision, even with my protective lenses, to a few feet.

Olivia shouts something, it sounds harsh and I assume its a curse. I get that. This is bad. We won't make it to the others. The storm is gaining distance.

Changing directions I run, carrying Olivia, straight into the wind. The gale force pushes back, I strain against it, digging my feet in to gain each step forward while being pushed backwards. Leaning into it, I make headway, but slow, too slow. My neck and shoulders knot into hard balls as I push forward.

I fold my wings in tight as the wind tries to catch and

force them open. The sand tears at me, ripping at our clothes. Olivia has small cuts on all her exposed skin, her lack of scales leaves her unprotected. I have to get her to safety.

Distant screams reach my ears. I yell too but the rush of the wind carries the sound of my voice away. The sandstorm is blinding. If I don't find shelter for us, Olivia might not survive.

My hearts pound harder. Adrenaline pumping fuels my rage. The bijass pushes in, trying to claim my mind. I can't let it.

The wind gusts and Olivia's cries of pain reach my ears over its gale force noise. Moisture streams from her tightly closed eyes. She turns and buries her face against my chest, seeking protection.

The rock outcropping is just ahead. Safety, shelter, I must reach it.

I get an idea, it's dangerous, but I have to protect her. The wind pushes hard but I open my wings. A gust catches them, pulling, straining my muscles.

It hurts, a lot.

Ignoring the pain I force them forward. It feels as if the muscles are tearing as I push my delicate wings against the wing.

I'm pushed back as I do. Sliding along the sand, my heels digging in deeper. At last they're closed around Olivia, protecting her from the worst of the storm.

Pushing ahead, I regain the lost ground as the intensity of the storm increases.

Darkness falls, the swirling dirt and sand blacking out the suns.

Every step is a triumph of will. Muscles tear as I force them beyond any demand I've put on them before. The ache in my wings fades under the onslaught of cutting sand. Olivia is shaking in my arms. We're almost to the rocks.

The wind blasts me backwards again, stealing what ground I've gained. Leaning forward I push back against the assault. One step, another, then sliding back. My feet press down, swaying my tail for balance, the sand comes half-way up my calves as I push my way forward.

Despite my protective lenses I can't see more than a few inches in front of my face. It's a swirling wall of grains of sand. The outcropping of rock appears as if materializing from nothingness, cutting through the storm for a moment. Putting the wall to my left I use its shelter to make my way along, looking for the crevice I noticed earlier.

The wind is whipping back and forth, pushing me away from the rock then slamming me into it. I keep myself turned out just enough so that when it slams me back, I can protect Olivia. The wind, sand, and debris pounds my shoulder and side with bruising force but it doesn't matter, I'm protecting her.

Feeling my way along the wall, at last I find the crevice. My wing muscles cry out in pain as I open them and then shove Olivia into the opening. She stumbles in to the tight space, safe, or safe as possible in the middle of a sand storm.

I can't fit all the way in, I'm too broad for the opening. It's fine as I use my body to block the storm from finding its way into her. It's not deep or wide, but there's enough room for her to be out of the worst of the storm. Her body presses close to mine and now, with relative safety, I can't take my attention off the feel of her soft curves.

My prime penis stirs, stiffening, pressing into her rear. Her scent fills my nostrils, an intoxicating odor that carries my thoughts away. I want her.

She leans into me, her head tilting up towards mine. On

impulse, feeling bold, I claim her lips as I have seen Astarot do with his female.

The storm fades to background noise, concern and pain wash away in the sweet release of her mouth.

I probe her lips with my tongue, exploring het depths. Her tongue darts out, meeting mine, a pleasure I've never experienced.

Her rear moves against my body, grinding, making my cock harder. I desperately want to fill her over and over until she screams my name in pleasure. Tasting her mouth ignites a desire to taste her lower.

Impossible in this cramped space. We're in a storm, separated from our group, lost in the wilds. It doesn't matter. She's giving herself and I want all she offers.

I will please her. I want her moaning. Sliding one arm over her shoulders, I move it down across her front over her soft, exposed breasts, so different than a Zmaj woman. I've dreamed of her soft flesh since meeting her. I wonder what they look like, feel like, what they would taste like in my mouth.

Ignoring them out of necessity and impossibility I slide my hand into her pants, seeking her core.

My fingers slide across soft fur then find wetness. Moving my hand around I find her opening, slick and ready, my finger slides easily inside. She moans into our kiss, the start of what I will make her feel.

I shove my finger as far inside her as I can then move it in a slow circle. Her rear grinds hard into my pounding cock. I groan, almost to the edge myself.

Sliding my finger in and out, her moan rises to match and overtake the whistling wind. She pants even louder as I pull my finger out and up, pressing into her body. A hard nub rubs against my finger and pressing it seems to bring her more pleasure, causing her to shiver and shove her body into me.

She wiggles under my ministration. My cock pounds with its need for release. Her wetness is enough to allow me to slide a second finger inside. She cries out and then she screams my name, pressing hard into me. Her body shudders in my arms, then she goes limp.

I hold her tight, keeping her safe while we wait for the storm to pass.

7

OLIVIA

I startle awake. It's quiet. Too quiet. I can't believe I fell asleep.

I'm stiff and sore. Everything aches as I try to get my bearings. A warm glow in my core reminds me of what happened, bringing a slow smile. Ragnar's reassuring presence presses against my backside.

"Ragnar?" I ask, unable to turn far enough to see him.

He stirs and says something. Sun streams down into the crevice he shoved us in during the storm. I don't know how long we've been here, but it feels like hours and hours. Maybe a day or more. How long does a sandstorm last? Ragnar's cool scales are nice, comforting, but he moves away and the heat of Tajss settles over like a heavy blanket.

Rock scrapes at my skin as I extract myself. As I turn to look around, sunlight reflects off the fresh-swept red sand, blinding me. My eyes water up as I squeeze them tight against the blinding pain.

Slowly they adjust, Ragnar is standing a small distance away.

I gasp. His back!

Ragnar's left wing hangs lower than it should, drooping oddly. Blood drips to the sand from dozens of cuts in his shredded skin, despite his protective scales.

I can't imagine what the storm would have done to me.

My face burns hot knowing he protected me from the worst of it. I've got minor wounds but they're nothing compared to how hurt he is.

Making my way over, I stumble in the sand and he turns around. The concern on his face brings tears. How can he be more concerned about me than his own pain?

Reaching him, I stretch my arms up to touch his face. His hand goes around my waist, then his other is on my cheek. He wipes away the first tear that falls, saying something in a soft whisper.

"I wish we could talk," I say, my voice soft to avoid it cracking.

The moment stretches out until at last he moves his hand from my face.

He turns, says something, then points into the distance. Looking over his shoulder at me when I don't respond, he repeats the same sounds.

"Sure," I agree, to what I have no idea.

It doesn't matter, I'll follow him to the ends of the earth.

Inhaling deeply, I let the breath out slowly, hoping to clear my head. It works, mostly, but I wish it hadn't. Taking a good look around, it hits me how screwed we are. There's no sign of the others and I'm lost.

Sand, nothing but sand with the occasional rock outcropping for as far as the eye can see stretches out to the horizon. No tracks, no shadow of people in the distance, nothing. Empty sand.

Hopefully Ragnar knows what direction to go.

Turning a circle, I hope to see my pack somewhere but there's nothing. I lost it in our struggle to make it through the storm. As hard as those winds were gusting it could be a thousand miles away.

"Damn it!" I scream, hands balling into fists.

Ragnar is at my side. His strong arms turn me as he enfolds me against his overly muscled chest. I press my face against his bulging bicep and lose the battle with my emotions. Tears fall and I'm sobbing, uncontrollable.

Lost to overwhelm.

Crashed on this planet that's killing me slowly from dehydration and heat exhaustion.

Everyone on my ship is dead or captured.

We're completely on our own, cut off now from all our friends.

I don't know how much time I waste but at last I'm cried out. Too dry for tears, empty, drained of everything.

Pushing off of his chest, my fingers linger on the one good thing left in the world. Ragnar lets me go but there's a reluctance to his grip like he doesn't want to either.

Inches apart, we stare into each other's eyes.

"What now?" I ask, hoping the idea somehow gets past the language barrier.

He tilts his head to one side, frowns- which furrows his brow in an absolutely adorable way, then says something. His language has so many soft sounds, drawn out S's that create a constant hissing, but it's soothing, not like I would associate with a snake or anything.

It's kind of sexy, in a strange way.

He turns half-way and points.

I shrug. That way looks as good as any. After all, what the hell do I know? I'm lost.

I nod my understanding and agreement then we walk.

We don't make it a hundred feet before it's clear how badly hurt Ragnar is. My first clue is that he isn't using his wings. The Zmaj are perfect for their environment. They use

55

their wings to move across the sand with ease despite their huge size and weight. They hardly sink into the sand at all, flapping their wings and using their tail to guide and balance themselves.

Ragnar doesn't open his wings at all, so he's sinking into the sand even worse than I do thanks to his bigger mass. With each step he sinks in almost to his knees, fighting for forward motion. His back is still bleeding, leaving a small trail of blood.

That can't be good. I have no idea how many hell-planet monsters can track by scent of blood.

We press on. What choice do we have?

We walk in silence, neither having the energy to spend on talking. We wouldn't understand each other, anyway.

The suns rise higher, baking us until at long last they drop in the sky. Ragnar looks worse. The bleeding stopped some time back, but he still isn't using his wings.

He hurt himself opening them to protect me from the storm.

For me.

The consequences of his actions overshadow the warm glow in my stomach.

He says something, looking down at me. My eyes are so dry that my eyelids grind like sandpaper when I blink until I can see clearly. He speaks again and I shake my head, shrugging my shoulders.

No idea what he's saying. This sucks.

He touches my face, turning it gently, until I'm staring out across the emptiness.

"What?" I ask.

He speaks again, points, then says more words. I blink a few more times and then it's there. In the distance is a shadow. It seems too far away to reach but it's the outline of something breaking the flatness of the horizon.

"What is that?" I ask, looking up to his eyes.

He doesn't understand so all he can do is take my hand as we resume walking. The suns drop lower, bringing a welcome bit of relief as the temperature drops from scorching to damn hot.

I'm focusing on one foot in front of the other. Every muscle hurts. Muscles I didn't know I had. My head is pounding with an increasing intensity. I'm parched, so dry I can't swallow. My lips are cracked too. Dehydration is settling in, an unwelcome old friend.

Ragnar says something that sounds like he's excited.

Raising my head takes an effort of will. When I do, what had been a distant shadow is now clear. Trees.

It must be a mirage. Or a fever dream. That must be it, I'm seeing things. Heat stroke can do that to you. I think.

Ragnar talks more so I smile. I'm just having some kind of mental break, it's okay. If I can put one foot in front of the other, things will be better.

Trees. What a joke.

Several steps later, I can't count how many, I bump into something hard.

It must be Ragnar. What else could I run into?

Again the massive effort to raise my head.

There's that damn tree again. This thing is huge! The base of it must be twenty feet around, maybe more. It rises straight up, growing thinner as it goes, for fifteen feet then massive branches stretch out. This is one hell of an illusion.

Reaching out, I touch it. The bark is cool with a rough texture and I lean closer, resting my face against it.

Ragnar grips my arm, pulling.

"Leave me alone, this is my illusion damn it," I mutter, but he's insistent.

Sighing, I let him pull me away. I know the tree will disappear when I stop touching it. My mind can only create this illusion for so long. But it doesn't go away. The tree is still there and Ragnar is pulling me past it. My foot touches down on ground that doesn't give way the moment I put my weight on it.

Grass! Yellow grass, but grass. It's been so long since I've seen grass! On the generation ship there were these huge, open parks with trees and grass and even simulated sunlight. I loved walking the paths of the park close to my dorm. It was a great place to go to be alone. I used to walk barefoot, letting the grass tickle my feet.

"Is this real?" I ask, then laugh, remembering an ancient song. "Is this the real life? Is this just fantasy?"

The entertainment loaded onto the ship's databases was all old stuff. I used to read about Earth and what it was like before my grandparents loaded onto the generation ship. The overcrowding of the planet forced most of the population to live underground, except for corporations and the very rich. They built the generation ships to reduce the population of Earth. They loaded them up with all they thought would be necessary to keep the passengers sane.

I'd never known life outside the ship, so for me it was home. Until we crashed here. Then the wreck was my home, but it's gone now, too.

"Trees!" I yell on a sudden whim.

I run over and hug a tree. It's too big to get my arms around, but pressing my face against the cool bark is so nice.

Opening an eye, Ragnar is watching me. He probably thinks I've lost my mind. Maybe I have. I mean, there are trees and grass. In the middle of the desert. That's crazy, right?

Ragnar says something then points.

"Sure!" I agree, as if I have a clue what he said.

It doesn't matter. I'm either crazy or happy. Either way it's better than what I've felt in a long time. Since before being kidnapped by those damn pirates.

I'll take it. Live in the moment right?

Ragnar waits until I'm by his side then we walk together. The trees are numerous but widely spaced, dozens of feet between each. It's like they're respecting each other's territory.

Between the trees is the weird yellow grass but there are other plants. Strange looking flowers with brightly colored foliage. We walk by a patch of flowers as tall as my waist that wave back and forth as we pass. They're pretty, a beautiful shade of purple. I reach out to touch them but Ragnar grabs my hand and stops me. He shakes his head side to side saying something stern.

"Sorry," I say.

He smiles a tight smile, reminding me how much pain he's in.

As we move through the trees, something splashes. Stopping, I look up at Ragnar.

"Water?" I ask, excitement rising.

It has to be, right? There'd have to be water for there to be trees and grass. An oasis?

Of course! I'm not going crazy!

I've seen these in movies. Deserts have these little islands where there's water and plants and life!

Ragnar touches my shoulder, jerking my attention. My smile is so wide it will split my face. We're going to live!

Grabbing Ragnar's hand, I pull forward, leading the way. Moving past one of the massive boles of a tree, the pond lays out before us like a piece of heaven pulled to earth. Crystal clear, shockingly blue water edges towards glittering turquoise. There's even a tiny waterfall at one end. It's not big, but it's beautiful.

We walk, hand in hand, into the water. It's cool, so

refreshingly cool. I know I should take my clothes off but I don't want to wait. The water rises the further in we walk until it's at Ragnar's waist, up to my chest.

The massive Zmaj hunter looks at me with hungry eyes, locked on my breasts that are lifted by the buoyancy of the water.

"Not yet," I say, shaking my head. "Turn around."

Grabbing him by his waist, I turn until his back is to me. It's a shredded mess. While it stopped bleeding a long time ago, the wounds are nasty. Dried blood is black along the open cuts filled with sand and grit. Where his wings connect to his back, the skin and scales are a deep, angry purple with a yellow tinge. The left is the worst, hanging off-kilter with black bruising.

"I need to clean these wounds," I say, touching his sides while carefully avoiding the worst damage.

His back tenses and his wings shift, but he doesn't move away.

Reaching down, I grab two handfuls of sand, having to duck my head under the water to reach it. Butterflies dance in my stomach as I reach towards him with the sand. This will hurt. There's no way around it.

Bracing myself for I don't know what, I place both hands on the top of his back. He hisses, jerking forward, his back muscles tensing.

"Sorry," I say, tears forming in the corners of my eyes.

He did this for me. All to protect me.

He doesn't move again or make any more sounds so I move my hands in slow circles, using the sand to scrub the wounds. The water running down his back turns red as crusty sand and other crap comes loose. I repeat the cycle over and over. Handfuls of sand, rub his back, aching inside with each touch. He hisses just every so often. A soft, pained sound that breaks my heart every time.

"Last one," I say, trying to sound soothing with at least the tone of my voice. "Just a bit more."

Something makes a cracking sound behind us, followed by a shriek. Ragnar whirls around so fast it knocks me off balance and I fall backwards into the water.

I'm under so fast I don't have time to take a breath. My lungs burn and panic rises. Swinging my legs and arms wildly, I try to determine up from down. Muffled screeches come clearer as I break the surface, gasping in air and treading water.

Ragnar is two feet ahead, his arms out wide and he hisses loud. On the land, facing him, is a creature.

It's a huge, gorilla-looking thing that pounds the ground with massive, tree-trunk arms. The earth trembles. Thick white fur hangs over its shoulders and down the top half of its arms, but the bottom half is bare skin that's a rich blue color. It has sharp brown eyes that stare right at Ragnar.

It screams, a loud, harsh sound that hurts my ears. The leaves of the trees rustle as if in response to its call.

My stomach tightens into a hard ball.

Cold chills run down my limbs.

A half dozen more of the things, smaller but still huge, drop out of the trees and move into a line just behind the big one.

"Shit," I exhale.

8

RAGNAR

I hiss and hit my chest then throw my arms wide. The majmun alpha rises onto his hind legs, answering my challenge.

It's a big one. Standing on two legs, he's not much shorter than me. He pounds his chest with a thumping sound that vibrates in my bones.

The rest of his pack lines up behind him, ready to support their leader. Olivia says something behind me that sounds like a curse. If I was armed and wasn't hurt, this wouldn't be the problem it is now. I'm unarmed and can't use my wings, this could go either way. majmun are primal and that calls to my bijass. I want to dominate the challenger.

The red rage rises, pushing for control. Nothing will stand against me.

Edicts. Remember the edicts.

Olivia says something and I wish, with all my heart, I knew what she was saying. The majmun alpha pounds the ground again, earth flying up from his fist. On a whim, I respond by slapping the water with my open hand. It sprays across the distance, soaking his thick fur.

He screeches and scampers back, baring his teeth at me. Smiling, I take two steps forward, hissing and holding my arms out to the side. He storms forward but stops before coming too close to the water's edge. He screeches, rises, pounds his chest then drops heavily to all fours.

Stepping forward another step, I slap the water, palms down, making a thunderous report. The majmun lined up to either side of him drop back, almost cowering. The alpha holds his ground but I sense his fear. So does his tribe. The smallest of them turns and leaps up into the branches of the nearest baoba tree.

I slap the water again, this time cupping my hands to send more water spraying at the alpha. He sees it coming and scampers back with a high-pitched shriek. He dodges the water spray, but he's lost esteem in the eyes of his tribe. The beta, a majmun every bit as big as the alpha, watches.

Suddenly, in a blur of motion, the beta leaps, landing on the alpha's back. The two of them roll into the tree line, out of sight. Sounds of a struggle ensue and the rest of the majmun look at each other, chittering and screeching. Almost as one they leap away into the tree-tops.

When I turn, Olivia is right behind me. Her wet shirt clinging to the curves of her body outlines the fullness of her unprotected breasts. Dark circles shine through the wet fabric at the center, hard points pressing through the fabric. My prime penis stiffens, pushing uncomfortable against the cloth of my pants.

Rage gives way to desire, still the influence of the bijass. I bested my foe and protected my female, now it demands I claim her. My cock throbs, pulsing with the beating of each of my hearts. Stepping closer to her, my erection presses into her stomach.

Her eyes widen, she looks down, then up with a shy smile. She speaks, words that have no meaning, no understanding.

It should be clear what I need, how can she not see? I want her.

She says something again then puts her hands on my shoulders and twists. Looking at her small, pale hand on my skin, I follow the beautiful line of her arm back to her face. She's speaking still and attempting to twist me around.

Curious what she is thinking, I move to her desire. She stops when my back is to her. There's a small splash as she goes under the water, then she's scrubbing my back with handfuls of sand again. Instinct rages with the pounding of the bijass, demanding satisfaction. I struggle with desire, no matter how strong the urge I will take nothing from her she does not freely offer.

Pushing past the urges allows me to focus on her touch. She's gentle but it hurts. Some of the wounds must be deep, judging by the depth of my pain.

Each time I flinch she says something that sounds like *eyemsosawry*.

Staring down at the water, it becomes tinted with red. I'm going to need healing paste. If we hadn't lost the group it wouldn't be a problem. I had packed some for our journey to the city.

Now, separated and alone, there is none. I'll have to make it. This would be fine if I wasn't already wounded. I try to open my wings. Everything turns white hot, blinding me with pain. Crying out, I lose my balance.

Her voice cuts through the splashing water and the agony. Her soft hands are on my face, cupping my cheeks. Concern and fear dance behind her beautiful eyes.

"I'm fine," I say, resting a hand on her waist to steady myself.

She says something and I curse our inability to talk. Her fingertips trail down my cheeks and I force a smile. Reassuring her I'm fine in the only way I can. My dick throbs with hard, pulsing need and desire to the point I might explode, spilling my desire into the water.

Gripping her waist in my hand as I wrap my free arms around her shoulders, I pull her closer. Holding her tight, crushing my steel-hard cock between us.

I'm in no shape to travel and she isn't either. We need rest and time to heal. I don't know how far from the city we are, or if I'm going in the right direction. We're here, together, and I need her. Desire pushes aside reasons I should do anything but hold her.

Her body molds to mine, fitting against me as if made for just this moment. Her soft, full breasts press into my chest. My prime penis digs into her stomach and as she moves and I'm almost pushed over the edge. Lowering my hands across her beautiful ass, I take it and squeeze, lifting her, pulling her face to mine.

Her head leans back.

Her lips part, welcoming.

Time slows, the small distance becoming a huge chasm.

Closer, my hearts beat, then closer.

My lips tingle in anticipation. I will mate with her mouth as Astarot has done with his female.

Closer.

Soft, luscious mouth pressing, moving against mine.

Cock pulsing.

Hands roaming.

My tongue darts out, tasting her.

9

OLIVIA

*H*is tongue touches my lips, the taste of him is cool and scorching all at once.

He pulls back, his eyes smoldering with desire. I'm left shaking, hollow.

My pulse throbs between my legs.

His hands are on my ass, roaming back and forth, his fingertips grazing between my legs. A shiver races up my spine.

One of his hands moves up my back to stroke my hair as he leans in.

His tongue darts out once more, licking, tasting, exploring.

I didn't know Zmaj knew what a kiss was, but damn he's good!

He runs his hand through my hair as his lips meet mine again. Soft, gentle kisses, our lips touch and part.

Wrapping my arms around his neck I let myself go, giving in to his touch. Panting through parted lips our tongues meet, dance then part.

Soft lips seeking more. My fingers tingle as I run them

down his neck and across his shoulders. His scales are cool to the touch, the hard silky texture enticing.

Ragnar trails his hand down my spine. Another shiver at its passage.

Still in the oasis, lapping waves of warm water caress between my legs. Desire pounds through my veins, drumming with my racing pulse.

The enormous Zmaj hunter carries me out of the water, his lips never far from mine.

His tongue darts in and out, like a hummingbird tasting a sweet flower.

I groan with pleasure.

His cock pressing into my stomach feels huge. Too big to believe. I want him but can my body handle that much?

Awareness beyond the sweet, cinnamon-ish taste of his lips is dim as he moves us out of the water.

Wrapping my legs tighter around his waist drives his cock so hard into me, I can feel it pulsing. He wants me.

He wants me.

I have to think it again.

I'm not the girl guys want, not like this. Ragnar doesn't care, he wants me. In his arms, I'm special.

Pleasure races out from deep in my center, making me shudder with the force of its passage.

I've never, in my life, felt desired like I do now.

We're lowering but it's like I'm floating. He's so strong, there's no sense of gravity. No pull of the earth. I'm in the embrace of his wings, drifting to the ground.

Ragnar covers me, large and powerful. His lips crushing mine.

On his elbows, engulfing me with his large size, I'm tiny and possessed.

His soft lips kiss across my cheek, his hands roam across my wet blouse.

I run my fingers through his hair, stroking along the bulky muscles of his shoulders down to his bulging biceps then back up and through his hair.

His cock strains against his pants, pressing hard against my pussy. Wet heat soaks my thighs. I wonder again how big can he actually be?

His thumb passes over my nipple, shock waves drive out all other thought.

Moaning in pleasure my hips move with a mind of their own, pushing up and into him.

In moments my blouse is off then his warm mouth encompasses my swollen nipple and I'm gasping for air.

His hot, rough tongue licks across then circles while he sucks. I flush as my heart jumps into overdrive.

Pleasure makes me writhe beneath him.

I'm transported under the ministrations of his tongue to my breasts. He moves from one to the other then back.

As he rises from one, he pauses and looks for a long, admiring moment.

He lowers his head and his mouth works one hard bud while his thumb and forefinger play with the other.

It's a double whammy of sensation.

My clit throbs so bad it almost hurts.

My hands tighten in his hair, pulling as the intense pleasure of his mouth wracks my body.

As he passes from one breast to another his hips grind against me. The bulge of his cock presses hard against my pussy even through our clothes.

I take one hand from his hair and slide it down between us.

I need release; the pressure is too much.

He moans against me, vibrating my breasts.

"Ragnar!" I cry out, my hand slipping inside my pants.

Passing down I find my swollen clit. The moment my

fingers touch, I buck underneath his greater weight, driving his cock hard against the dividing fabric.

Shudders race through me, my toes curl and my back arches.

His bulky arms wrap around me, protective, pulling me to his chest and holding me close.

My orgasm spikes in a quick, overwhelming snap.

It eases just as quickly and I know it wasn't enough. I need him more.

Ragnar kisses down the swell of my breasts and onto my stomach.

A moment of self-consciousness passes over me but washes away as he kisses his way lower. His fingers stroke hot trails of fire down my sides. They hook under the hem of my pants and I lift, letting him slide them off.

He hisses as I'm exposed, his eyes widening in clear admiration.

His hands move slowly, tentative, and I would almost swear they tremble just before he touches me.

He runs his hands over my middle and down my thighs, lowering his head.

His tongue darts out and touches me at the top of my opening making me shiver in anticipation.

Large, firm hands push apart my thighs, demanding entrance.

His warm breath crosses my delicate lips and his hands lightly massage my thighs, then his tongue traces the crease of my leg, just touching the left side of my lips.

My eyes roll back in my head with pleasure. Grabbing his hair in both hands I knot my fingers and tug, pulling him towards my center.

His rough, hot tongue laps at the outside of my folds without penetrating.

Delicate, rapid licks, tasting my juices, he groans and says something. God I wish I knew what it was but it sounds so breathtakingly sexy!

Lowering his head his tongue drives in and I cry out as its rough width forces me open.

He drags it up, moving side to side, opening me to my fullest.

Pulling up until he reaches my clit, he encompasses it with his mouth and sucks.

I've never felt anything like this. My limbs go weak, my muscles are unresponding jelly.

Fire burns through my veins.

My heart races like wild horses.

I rise to the edge then he backs me down, moving from my center, licking my thighs, my outer lips and then somehow sensing I'm off the edge he drives back in, pushing me back up before retreating again.

It's a roller-coaster of sensation. Rising, cresting, then backing away.

His hands are everywhere, touching, exploring as his tongue searches me out.

I'm taken by a storm. Falling into my orgasm, a tightness in my core that explodes. I'm washed away. Waves of fiery pleasure burn through my limbs then ice comes behind.

My back arches, my toes curl as I lift into him and beyond.

He holds me tight as my body shudders, I'm in his strong arms.

Shivering, the last vestiges of my pleasure pass. My muscles twitch before I collapse to the ground, protected by the warmth of his body.

He climbs up, passing over me, until our lips meet again. Soft gentle kisses.

One of his hands lowers while he holds himself up with

the other. Anticipation tinged with fear creates a thrill that rushes through me.

I've wondered so many times what he looks like, how big can he be? Now, at last, I'm going to find out.

Fumbling, he undoes his pants until they hang loose. Deep in shadow I catch a swinging glimpse of a massive cock.

It can't be that big!

He slides his pants down and his dick bounces free.

Its massive, and it's ridged. It's too big. I panic and push against his chest, sliding away.

He looks up, meeting my eyes, confusion dancing in his.

Shaking my head side to side I can't take my eyes off his cock.

It's as big around as my fist and the top side has ridges that look like they're made of bone running from the head to the base. And long! It has to be over thirteen inches.

"I can't," I say. "It's too big!"

Pushing my way out from under him, I reach for my clothes. He says something, shaking his head, and I know he doesn't understand. How do I make myself understood?

He rolls back onto his knees. His massive, thick, rock-hard cock juts out like an accusing finger.

I can hear the question in his voice even if I don't understand the words. Shaking my head, I point at his cock then make a circle with my hands, mimicking its size. Pointing at my own parts I shrink the size of my hands, shaking my head.

Ragnar frowns.

I feel terrible but what if he hurts me? We're lost in the desert with no one else around. I can't, not here, not now.

He says something else, stands up and pulls his pants back into place.

"I'm sorry," I say.

Useless words.

He looks at me for a long moment. There's no accusation in his eyes but he turns his back and walks a distance off. Pulling my clothes on, I put my back to one tree and wrap my arms around my knees. How can I be so terrible?

10

RAGNAR

*T*he suns drop to the horizon, stretching their final, red rays through the leaves of the baboa trees. I feel out of place.

Why did Olivia push me away?

What did I do wrong? Did I fail to please her?

The sweet taste of her is on my tongue and I would happily continue if more is what she wants.

Sunlight sparkles off the oasis and some small, aquatic creature breaks the surface, causing a soft splash.

My awareness of Olivia has not dulled, my cock still aches for her. I want her. I need her and I'm certain I brought her pleasure. How different can these females be from Zmaj? Their anatomy is similar enough.

Though the way her breasts... how enticing and overtly sexual...

Sighing, I turn back to her. A war is not won by inaction.

Olivia trembles as our eyes meet. Beads of moisture dot her forehead as her eyes dart away.

I think I understand.

Walking over to her I place a hand gently on her cheek. Her eyes slowly rise to mine.

"I am sorry I was not pleasing to you," I say. "I will learn and be better."

She doesn't respond for a few moments then says something. One delicate eyebrow arches up as she tilts her head.

Not understanding what she is saying, I smile in what I hope conveys reassurance. She waits as if expecting me to respond and the moment drags out, but then she wraps her arms around me, lying her head on my chest.

No matter what might be wrong between us, nothing else matters but having her in my arms. A deep, fulfilling sense of satisfaction pleases the dragon in me.

This. This is what I want. Her. My treasure.

It doesn't matter how I have her, just that I do.

The shadows slide in as we stand, holding one another.

Words, impossible as they are, are unnecessary.

Running my fingers through her hair, the warmth of her cheek on my chest, this is all I need. The world will wait.

As darkness encroaches further, she stirs, pulling her face from my chest. She looks up and opens her mouth to say something when her belly grumbles. Her eyes widen as both her hands fly to her stomach. In the dim light her cheeks turn a brighter shade of red.

I understand her body. She's hungry.

Setting to work, I gather pieces of wood from loose limbs lying about and dry grasses. Using small stones, I surround a shallow pit and place the grass in the center then criss-cross the pieces of wood over it. Opening my mouth, I pull on the glands in my throat and spit a small ball of fire into my creation. The grass catches and the wood follows, making a small fire that will warm the guster meat in my pack. Also, it will keep most creatures at bay during the night.

There's less meat in the pack than I hoped. I'll have to

figure that out soon but we have enough for a few days. Acid roils in my stomach at concern for our survival. One day at a time. One moment at a time. The only way a hunter survives is to be in the moment.

Spreading your attention to worries will get you killed.

I spear five pieces of meat on a stick then hold them over the fire and rotate. Olivia watches with a small smile on her face. She's so beautiful, The way the firelight sparkles in her eyes ignites desire and a longing so deep it's as if it's in my bones.

Juices from the meat rise to the surface then drop, sizzling into the fire. Olivia's stomach grumbles again as the odor fills the air. I pull the stick back then offer it to her. She takes a piece off then tosses it back and forth between her hands, blowing on it. I hadn't considered how hot it might be or that it would be a problem for her.

"I'm sorry," I say, instinctive and automatic.

She looks up and I know she didn't understand what I said. It pains me, like a stab goring into my guts. She says something and damn it, if only I could understand her words.

She smiles then nibbles at the scorched meal. I take one off for myself, popping it in my mouth and chewing slowly while I watch her. Even the way she eats is delicate, soft, and somehow sensual. The curve of her lips as she chews calls me, enticing. My lips tingle with a desire to kiss her. A touch of juice slips down her chin when she takes a bite. I'm leaning forward before I realize it, intending to lick it but I stop myself.

She pushed me away. I don't know what she wants and I won't take anything from her she does not freely give.

She finishes her portion so I offer her another that she takes with a smile and more strange, hard words. Her language contrasts sharply with the softness that is her.

We eat, taking our time, I let her have three of the five pieces of meat. I can go days without food or water but she needs the traces of epis to help her body survive the heat. I also want to stretch the small supply we have as far as I can.

Darkness grips the world outside the small light of our fire by the time we finish. Olivia's eyes are heavy and she yawns. I haven't made a shelter for us but I think we'll be fine for tonight.

She rises and looks around then over at me. Smiling I stand up too and point at a thick patch of grass. She nods and goes over to it. I don't follow her, unsure of what she wants. The curve of her body, her rear, her hips distract me as she kneels. Looking over her shoulder she says something.

"I don't understand," I reply, shrugging a shoulder.

She frowns then holds a hand up and motions me over. My hearts leap into my throat. Walking over to her, the distance between us is like a long tunnel. Everything I desire is on the far side, if I can just make it through. She pats the ground behind her then lies down.

This I understand. Lying down behind her, she snuggles in close. I wrap an arm over her and curl my legs and tail, encircling her in my body. Her beautiful rear presses hard against my stomach. The throbbing of my cock makes sleep slow to come, but eventually it finds me.

I WAKE BEFORE OLIVIA DOES. THE STEADY RISE AND FALL OF her chest beneath my arm is peaceful. The first rays of the suns are peeking through the canopy of baboa trees. The rustle of leaves and the distant cry of majmun fills the air.

Olivia stretches, pressing back, and my cock stiffens against her sensuous rear. She rolls over on her side, facing me and says something. The expression on her face seems happy and on impulse, I kiss her.

I meant it to be a quick kiss, but the moment our lips touch, passion burns white hot. Her soft lips against mine awakens deep desire. Her hand runs down my side, trailing hot fingers along my scales. She bites my lower lip as I drive my tongue in, seeking hers.

Running my hands over her hips, down her legs, I hold her close to my body.

She's beautiful.

Her fingers move to my back and there's a sudden, sharp, stabbing pain. I pull back, suppressing a groan from the sudden and surprising pain.

The moment is broken.

Olivia's concern is clear as she leaps up leans across so she can see my back. The wounds burn. I was paying no attention to it, being caught up in her, but I know something is still not right.

She gasps, confirming my thoughts.

When she leans back she talks, rapid-fire, words flying out of her mouth, none of which I understand.

"It's okay," I say, but I know she doesn't understand my words anymore than I do hers.

I need healing paste. Which means we should get moving. It's obvious the wounds I suffered are getting infected. The paste will handle the problem but how do I tell her that?

Standing, I take her hands and pull her to her feet. She's still talking while I grab our bags and my spear. She grabs my arm, pulling until I turn and meet her eyes. Moisture gathers at the corners. She says something more and I shake my head.

A bead of the water from her eyes trails down her cheek and I wipe it away.

"Do not worry," I say, hoping my words will carry my intention even if they aren't understood. "Come."

I take her hand and then pull her along with me through the oasis. It doesn't take long before I spot a cvet. The first component I need to make healing paste. Turning to Olivia, I grip both her arms and point at the ground then wave a finger in front of her face.

"Stay here," I say. "Don't move. Stay."

Maybe if I only use simple words and gestures, she will understand. I hope. Cvet are dangerous but I've done this hundreds of times. Even as wounded as I am, a cvet is not a big threat. As long as she stays out of the way.

She nods but her lips tremble. Still feeling impulsive and not sensing any resistance, I steal another kiss. My hearts leap into overdrive at the simple touch.

Her finger tips linger on my cheek as I step away and the warmth of her touch stays with me as I turn to face the cvet.

It must sense our presence. A tremor runs through its leaves before I approach.

Whirling my spear, the red suns flash off the sharp tip. Stopping with it held two-handed over my head, I run and leap at the cvet. Almost I spread my wings, it's natural to do so, but the moment I start, I have to stop. The twinge of pain is enough to tell me how bad that would be.

Even without my wings, I get good air and my leap carries me to the center of the cvet. As gravity pulls me back down, I aim my spear right at the eye of the plant. Landing hard, I drive the point down. The plant thrashes in shock and pain. Vines and large leaves rise, lashing out, but I push my spear in deeper.

Olivia cries out. Out of the corner of my eye I catch her standing where I told her, eyes wide, both hands covering her mouth.

One vine slashes my face, its sharp edge hitting the

overlap of my scales and cutting through. The cvet's poison burns deep into my jaw. Hissing in pain and anger I twist my spear and it gives a final shudder before dying.

I hate these damn plants. I'd never mess with them if it wasn't for the healing paste.

The effort of killing the cvet leaves me worn. My back burns and the cut on my face is pulsing fire with every beat of my hearts. Breathing heavily, I climb out of the center of the plant and walk over to Olivia.

"Are you okay?" I ask.

I look her over for wounds, making sure she is unharmed. I'm thankful that she listened and stayed where I told her. Having interacted with Lana, I'm sure that female would not have listened. She'd have run in and caused a problem while trying to help. My treasure is much smarter.

"Good," I say, finishing my review of her well-being.

She stays close while I harvest the sap from the plant's large leaves. After I do one, she motions to the small knife in my hand. I give it to her and she carefully takes another leaf and duplicates what I just did.

She's slower and not as smooth, but she does it correctly. My smile stretches from ear to ear. She's not only beautiful, but she's smart and able too. Any male in the galaxy would be proud of a mate like her.

I finish sealing the jar and take great care packing it in the small bag we kept through the storm. Now I need sismis teeth. Sismis are nocturnal, so entering their caves is best done during the day when they are not active. There are normally caverns not far from an oasis if I can find one.

As I heft our pack onto my shoulder, Olivia takes my free hand placing hers in it. Her warm skin is soft, at her merest touch I'm consumed by desire and need.

She is my treasure and soon I will have her writhing again with pleasure and she will beg me to claim her.

Leading us out of the oasis, I set a pace she can manage. Once we're clear of the trees, I scan the land for signs. It isn't long before I notice the small details I want. A rocky outcropping of pushed up ground. Large boulders rising to dominate the sand. A good place to look for a cave entrance.

Olivia pushes herself to move faster. When we started she talked, almost non-stop, but it's been over an hour and she's now fallen silent, moisture pouring down her face, panting with every step.

We reach the rough, rocky area. None of them are tall, nothing coming higher than my shoulder. I weave us through them until I find an opening into the ground. Good, just what I had hoped for.

"I will go down into the cavern," I say, taking both her hands in mine. "Come over here."

I lead her a dozen feet away from where I'll be going into the cave. It's next to one of the bigger boulders and should be safe, or as safe as anything in Tajss is. I motion again while talking as I did last time. It worked then so I hope she will understand again what I want.

She nods her head but there is fear in her eyes. I have no way to fix that but it weighs heavy on me as I return to the cave entrance.

It's nothing more than a black hole in the ground. Lying flat and peering in, it's about a ten foot drop. Getting back out may be difficult without my wings to assist. I climb back to my feet and go to the other side of the hole then lie down again and look at it from this angle.

There's my way out. The cavern wall is only a couple of feet in from this angle. I'll be able to climb up it, then I should be able to either reach the edge of the hole or leap and make a grab for it.

Decision made, I turn and hang my legs over the edge.

Checking on Olivia one last time, I twist and drop, grabbing the edge as I fall then lower myself to the ground.

I have to drop the last couple of feet.

Landing in a three point crouch I wait, listening to make sure I haven't created a disturbance. A soft rustling sound drifts through the air then silence.

My eyes adjust to the dimmer light. Sismis cover the ceiling, clinging to it. Good, finding what I need should be no problem.

The winged creatures grow new teeth throughout their life to replace old ones. They shed their teeth like a baboa tree sheds leaves. Discarded fangs cover the ground of their nest, mingled with excrement and all I have to do is sift through their dung until I find enough for what I need. Now to make my way back to the entrance.

My back and wings scream in pain as I climb my way up the wall. Ignoring the discomfort I pull myself higher. Almost to the entrance, just a little more.

Stretching my fingers, I just reach the opening but I can't get a grip.

I'm going to have to jump for it.

Damn.

This will hurt.

Closing my eyes, I take several deep breaths, preparing myself. I open them and leap without further thought. My wings want to spread, my body operates on instinct too deep to be under my total control. I stop them before they open, but even the attempt is painful.

My fingertips catch the lip of the cave entrance. I'm hanging, swinging back and forth, then pull myself up.

My head comes above ground again and Olivia is standing just where I told her too.

She beams and waves.

The ground trembles beneath my hands. It's faint, just enough I notice it.

Fear grips my stomach in a tight knot. It can't be a zemlja, nothing worse could happen right now.

Scrambling, I rush to pull myself over the edge but as I do, cracks form in the ground between Olivia and I.

Strange.

I look up at Olivia just in time to see the ground open underneath her. Her scream cuts through the air driving straight into my hearts.

11

OLIVIA

*A*s his head rises above the ground, relief makes my knees weak. If anything happened to Ragnar, I don't know what I'd do. I know it's more than how screwed I'd be surviving on this hellhole of a planet by myself. I care about him.

"Hi," I say, waving.

He looks down, digging into the loose sand and pulling himself further out. When he looks up again, his face is different. Concern? Fear?

"What's the matt-"

Before I can finish the sentence the ground beneath my feet disappears.

A sick feeling grips my stomach as I hang for what seems like a small eternity. Gravity is taking forever to do its thing, I'm like that coyote in the cheesy old cartoons when he walks off the cliff.

I look around, trying to figure out a way to save myself.

Short of growing wings and flying there's nothing.

Time speeds up in a rush and I'm falling, head over heels, tumbling.

Dirt and debris bounces off of me. The light is there, then gone, then there again.

Slamming into the ground knocks my breath away. I can't inhale. My lungs refuse to inflate.

Tears stream down my face. I'm hurt. I don't know how bad, it doesn't matter, though, if I can't breathe!

Air!

Gasping, trying, must inhale.

Work!

Air comes in with a sudden rush, bringing welcome relief.

Focusing on breathing keeps the panic at bay.

I fell.

A long way, too. It's dark. Why is it dark?

Fear fades into pain. Each breath hurts. I take several more minutes to decide I haven't punctured a lung. I think I'm only bruised.

"Ragnar?" I ask.

I keep my voice low but still it echoes back.

Shifting dirt and debris slide away from my body. It takes a moment, but I work myself to a sitting position.

"Ragnar?" I say again.

Something clicks then hisses. Cold, icy fear drives my eyes wide as I clench my jaw shut in response. I sense more than see movement in the dark, just beyond my sight. Goosebumps form on my skin and the hair on the back of my neck stands up.

Fear is paralyzing.

Dirt and rock shifts. Dust falls from above, filling the light with dancing motes that swirl and obscuring my vision.

My eyes are too slow to adjust to the dimmer light.

Movement. I'm sure of it. Just outside the brightness. Shadows shift as a shape leaps out, flying forward, and I scream.

My throat tears with the force.

I scramble backwards, terror erasing thought.

Teeth. Sharp, shiny, hundreds of teeth fly at my face.

My arms come up to cover myself, ineffective protection.

My feet scrabble, pushing back and away from the threat.

It hisses, snapping its maw.

The light from above disappears.

A loud cry, almost a threatening hiss, then motion.

I can't process what's happening. There's a blur of action. The teeth that are in my face, an inch away from snapping shut, fly backwards and disappear.

Screams, not mine, cut the air with razor sharpness making my ears ring. Panting, struggling to catch my breath, my stomach is a tight knot of acid.

Something moves behind me. Leaping from my backside to my feet, I jump back into the light.

This time I see it, or part of it. It's a lizard looking thing with a scaly snout filled with sharp teeth. Yellow eyes gleam and reflect the harsh light from outside the cavern.

It leaps.

As I drop, trying to dodge its deadly intent, something moves over my head.

The thing stops in mid-air. A hand is on its throat, gripping tight.

It struggles, sharp talons scrabble, trying to tear at the arm holding it off the ground. The hand at its throat tightens then twists in a single hard motion and there's a dull snapping sound.

The thing falls still, and the hand lets go.

An arm wraps around me, pulling me to my feet and encircling me.

Ragnar holds me against his chest, protected in the crook of his arm. He turns a circle, holding me close, his other hand held out ready for anything.

Soft clicks and hisses emerge from the shadows. There are more creatures out there.

Ragnar says something, pulling me along as he continues to turn a slow circle.

"What?" I ask.

He repeats himself, or I think he does. It sounds the same but I still don't understand what he wants.

He places a hand on my shoulder and pushes down. I comply, an unspoken command communicating his desire. Once I'm on my knees he takes his hand away then walks a full circle around me, staring into the darkness.

Clarity hits me with a suddenness that is breath taking. Gone is the fear, goosebumps, and the cold chills. Ragnar is here and I know, with a certainty that is bone deep, everything will be fine.

Three times he completes a circle. Outside the light is the sound of sharp claws clicking on stone, hissing, and the snapping of teeth but I watch Ragnar.

He's in his element and it shows. A smile plays across his lips, his eyes dance with light, he's excited. Muscles ripple as he moves like a cat. Crouching, turning, his tail swings side to side. My heart rate soars with desire. He steps forward then back, moving to the side then with a speed that is a blinding blur, he moves out into the shadows.

My throat tightens with fear. Sounds of a struggle ensue as I strain my eyes to see. His tail is in the light, then his back moves in from the darkness.

"RAGNAR!" I scream, pointing as another monster leaps from the side.

It's almost to him.I can't move, can't do anything, there's no time. It's going to reach him, sharp teeth will tear at him and I'll lose him!

His hand darts into the light and grabs the monster before it reaches him.

Bulging biceps flex, muscles ripple as he lifts the monster that must weight three or four hundred pounds up into the air, holding it there while it struggles to break free. Teeth gnash, claws thrashing the air, desperate to find purchase in Ragnar's flesh.

Ragnar steps back into the light. He has another monster held at bay in his other hand. The wounds on his back have torn open and blood pours, dripping down and off of his tail, pooling on the ground.

His strength on full display, he lifts the two creatures out to arm's length. They hiss as their teeth snap open and shut. Ragnar screams out loud, a battle cry that ignites hope, then he slams the two monsters together, smashing their skulls.

They're stunned by the impact and go limp in Ragnar's grip. He drops one to place both hands on the other. He twists and there's a dull snap. Crouching while keeping his eyes out into the shadows, he does the same to the other.

My heart pounds in my chest. I'm light-headed. Such a display of strength ignites a fiery passion in my soul like I've never felt before.

Ragnar steps out of the light and moves around in the shadows. Fear tinges desire with an icy chill until he reappears in the light.

Kneeling, he takes my face in his hands, staring into my eyes.

Our connection is stronger than ever. I feel his concern and fear for me.

Touching his face with the tips of my fingers I try to convey that I'm okay.

"Thank you," I say, trailing my finger tips along his cheek then down his neck and across his shoulders.

His lips spread into a smile and he leans closer, taking a kiss.

Fire burns through my veins, desire pulses with my heart. His touch is cool on my hot skin.

A shudder runs down my spine as his kiss brings sweet freedom. Free from fear, worry, and a gateway to desire.

My hands roam over his chest, hard muscles flexing while he holds himself in for our kiss. As my hands move up and over his shoulders I touch something wet, breaking the moment.

"You're hurt!" I exclaim, pulling back from the kiss.

He shakes his head, like he understood, then leans in for another kiss.

"No!" I say, shaking my head. "You're hurt, let me see."

Ignoring me or not understanding, he leans in again but I push back.

"I mean it, you're hurt," I say, climbing onto my knees.

My back and butt hurt, bad. I'm sure nothing broke but I think my bruises have bruises. It's nothing compared to Ragnar. Holding him by his shoulders so he will stay in place, I stand and move behind him.

The sight of his back makes me gasp.

Blood is seeping out of dozens of wounds reopened in his fight to save my life. Helplessness almost overwhelms me. I don't have any water or any way to care for him.

"Oh Ragnar," I say, tears welling.

He shrugs as he turns to face me. A tear slips out to fall down my cheek, and he wipes it away with his thumb. I try to look away, embarrassed at my tears and my inability to help. He places a hand under my chin and forces me to look up into his eyes.

He smiles, washing away all my concerns. My hand goes to his face, and he covers it with his own. Turning his head, he kisses the tips of my fingers.

It's a beautiful, perfect moment that drags on for I don't know how long. Time doesn't matter as long as I'm with him.

His hand resting on mine trembles. A small shiver, almost unnoticeable, except his eyes roll up, his eyes lids flutter, then he drops to the ground in a heap.

RAGNAR

a deep, throbbing pain pulses through my mind as awareness creeps in.

"Olivia!" I cry, leaping to my feet.

Curse the pain, where is she!

Spinning on my heel, she rushes into my arms before I can complete the motion. Her soft breasts press to my chest, her arms encompass me, her body molds to mine. Wrapping her in my embrace, the rush of fear for her safety recedes, letting the pain return.

Her head leans back, her soft eyes meet mine. Her heart beats against my chest, reassuring and comfortable.

I don't know how long I was out. The loss of blood must have overcome me. Dead guster lie in a heap outside the circle of light from the ceiling where she fell.

She's fine. Watching her fall, I'd never been more scared in my life. Running for her but knowing there was no way I could reach her in time. It was one of the most awful experiences I've ever had.

We hold each other for some time.

Long enough I grow tired. I need a few days to heal even

with the paste. My inability to use my wings is dangerous and makes travel harder.

Looking around the cavern she fell into, I decide this might be a good place to pass time.

The guster that made it their nest are dead, which also means meat and leather. If they were living down here, there has to be a way out.

Walking over to the walls of the cavern I run a hand along them. They're smooth and rounded, a safe place. We'll stay here until I can heal. Now how do I tell Olivia?

Turning back to her, she's staring up at the hole where she fell. She looks as I come over.

"We will stay here," I say, hoping maybe she'll just get it.

The confused look on her face is too easy to read. I couldn't be so lucky. I frown as I think about how to convey what I want to say.

I point to my back then to a spot next to the wall. She follows my motions but it's clear she's not understanding. I mime motions of sleeping then point to the spot by the wall again. Her brow furrows. An adorable dimple forms between the fur over her eyes.

When I point to my back again then repeat the other motions her eyes widen and her mouth forms an O. She got it!

She nods her understanding bringing a smile to my face.

I retrieve our pack from where I dropped it and dig through. I find the jar of juice we harvested from the cvet then pull the sismis teeth out of my side pouch. More searching and I find the small bowl I use to grind the teeth and set to work. Olivia watches with avid interest. It's obvious she's memorizing every motion.

Before long I have a supply of healing paste. I hold it out to her and point to my wings and back. She takes it, looking solemn. I give her my back and try not to tense when she applies the paste. It hurts but the pain soothes under the balm of the salve.

Once she's finished, I reseal the jar and pack it carefully away. Holding my arms out to her, we settle down next to the wall and I fall asleep, letting the salve do its work.

THREE DAYS.

This morning I opened my wings for the first time since the storm. It hurt, blindingly bad, but at the same time it felt good. I've been feeling like a cripple without them.

I'm not ready to travel but that's okay. It's been nice having time with her. I've shown her how to harvest guster meat and we built a smoking pit to preserve it.

Now we're harvesting the leather. We won't be able to take it all with us but I hate leaving anything to waste. It goes against the code of a hunter.

Maybe we can come back for it.

Olivia is turning the stretched hide over when I turn around. She's bent at the waist and her beautiful ass is pointing at me. Stepping closer I slap her ass with a light, playful tap.

She turns, exclaiming, but her smile is welcoming. Rising onto her toes she offers me her lips which I take without hesitation.

My prime penis stiffens, the heavy weight of it presses between us.

She moves in closer against my chest. Gripping her ass I lift her off her feet and her legs wrap around my waist. Shifting, I move her so that the head of my pulsating cock is between her legs. Desire and need consume all thought.

Her tongue drives into my mouth, tackling my tongue.

She's aggressive, demanding, and I want to give her all she wants and more.

If only she'll have me.

The sting of rejection colors my desire. This is more than we've done since I tried to please her with my mouth and she pushed me away.

Will she do so again?

"You are my treasure," I say, when we break for air.

She is, everything. All I want and need is her.

I carry her the short distance to the wall, pressing against it and holding her up with my hips to free my hands. Her fingers twine in my hair as our mouth mating continues.

The tiny clasps that hold her shirt closed are hard to work with my fingers but they give way at last, exposing her sweet skin.

Sliding my hands inside the cloth I cup her breasts. The weight of them in my hands makes my dick jump with tension, ready to explode its pent up desire.

Need. Pounding with every beating of my hearts.

My hips rotate, as if of their own accord, grinding my cock against her covered pussy.

Our tongues intertwine, tasting, exploring but it's not enough. I want more. I need more.

Lowering us down, I lay her on the ground beneath me. My hand slides down from her full breasts to the hem of her pants. Sliding under and into the dividing cloth, I find her soft fur and her wetness covers my finger.

She moans into my mouth.

My cock is pounding. It pulses, aching with unreleased need.

The cloth of her pants restricts my movement but I work a finger inside her. Her hips wriggle as she gasps, her eyes half closed. She bites her lower lip, nodding her head up and down.

"Mhmmm," she moans, as I drive my finger in and out.

Her hands go to her pants, sliding them down over her hips.

Licking her lips, I drive my tongue deep into her mouth just as I drive my finger into her.

She cries pleasure into my mouth and I take it.

Sliding in and out until she bucks her hips up and down to meet my finger, I push a second in.

I'm preparing her. I need her but I won't hurt her. I need to know her body can take the girth of my cocks. Even among Zmaj I'm large, and I wonder if that's not why she pushed me away.

My free hand is on her chest, flicking and playing with the hard nub at the top of her soft mounds. My tongue dances with hers.

Two fingers drive in and out of her wet pussy until she's taking them as easy as the first. Only then do I add the third. It's tight, so I move slow.

"Are you okay?" I ask, knowing she won't understand the words but she'll get my question.

She nods, panting.

I push my three fingers in her soft folds. Holding them there, I wait until she nods then slide them out in slow motion. Feeling every ridge and crevasse of her beautiful body. When just the tips are inside, I slide them back in.

Wetness soaks my fingers as her body warms to the pleasure I bring.

She moans, loud, her enjoyment echoing off the stone walls.

My hard cock throbs.

I want to bury myself inside her. But doubt niggles behind the urges.

Will she accept me?

Twisting my wrist as I slide in and out increases her pleasure.

She's panting, her hips make small thrusts up and down rising to meet me.

Bijass comes, threatening rational thought.

Desire, all consuming, need for her.

My cock pounds with the need for release.

Breaking from her lips, I trail my way down across her cheek then her slender neck.

She rises to meet my lips as I taste her sweet skin.

Trailing my tongue across her I move lower. Across her large breasts, teasing each of the hard nubs at their peak.

"Mmm," she sighs, pushing her chest up and into my mouth.

I enclose as much of her as I can take. Lavishing her with my tongue, nibbling and pulling with my teeth.

My fingers still slide in and out of her wetness.

Her hands run along my shoulders, pulling my hair.

Working my way lower and lower until at last I'm almost to her sweet opening. Inhaling her scent, the tight wound spring in my core explodes. I can't hold back. My need to taste her, to have her, is too strong for more foreplay.

Driving in, I lick her opening with my tongue. The small, hard button at the top of her rises to meet me. Lapping at her hard nub with my tongue, she screams my name.

Her fingers twine in my hair, pulling, making the experience more erotic.

I can't stop. She fills my senses, taste, touch, smell, pouring into me and I can't get enough. I want more of her.

Her hips thrust up as her back arches. Driving my fingers in deep, I curl them up and hold deep inside her, barely wiggling them. Pressing my tongue against her hard nub as her body is wracked with pleasure. She's beyond words, panting meaningless sounds as her pleasure grips her tight.

She shudders again and again. Muscles spasm under the contractions of her orgasm. Holding myself to her, I wring every last ounce until at last she collapses.

She lies back, panting, her chest rising and falling in rapid movements.

Pulling my head back then sliding my fingers out she gasps and shudders once more. I move up beside her, putting an arm and a leg across her.

My massively hard cock presses into her side as I lie and wait, letting her make the next move. Never would I force more on her than she wants, now it is up to her if she wants me.

13

OLIVIA

That was the most intense orgasm I've ever had in my life, which is saying something since the last time he made me come was the most intense too.

Ragnar is an incredible lover. Attentive, caring, delicate and rough at just the right moments. He moves up and lies beside me, one arm across my middle and his leg laid over mine. His huge cock digs into my side, massive is an understatement.

I want him.

I need him to take me, to claim me.

I'm going to do this.

Or at least try. I don't know if my body can handle him. He's so… big and ridged. Don't forget the ridges.

But I know he will never hurt me. If I can't handle it, he'll stop. He'll understand. I know he will.

Catching my breath as the last vestiges of my orgasm pass, I turn my head and kiss him. Soft, gentle kisses.

My hand trails along his side.

His hard, lightly scaled body is a pleasure to touch. Reaching his hips I trail my fingers over the lower part of his sculpted, lean abs and down across those muscles. I don't know the term for them and not all men have them but Ragnar does and my god do they turn me on. Those hard line muscles that dive from his abs down to where you know there's a beautiful cock.

He pulls back from my kiss, looking into my eyes and arching an eyebrow. Biting my lip, I nod to his unspoken question.

"Yes," I say. "Slow. We'll go slow."

He seems to understand.

The tie of his pants falls free and I slide my hand inside the cloth, continuing to trace the line of his muscles.

I can't suppress a shudder when my fingers find his cock.

It's so damn big!

Hard, pulsing, ready to go if only I can take it.

Running my fingers from the base of his shaft to the top I let the tips trail lightly along. Ragnar groans, his eyes rolling up into his head.

The underside of his cock is silky suede.

Up and down I move my fingers. Reaching the top, I find hints of his stickiness as his dick jumps under my touch. He groans my name and slick desire pools between my thighs.

His hips make the smallest of thrusts back and forth and I know his desire for me is overwhelming. Palpable. It makes me feel bold.

Nibbling his lower lip I stroke his cock faster.

I kiss my way from his lips down to his chest. Muscled, rippling with strength, a marble sculpture of perfection brought to life. Tracing the bulging lines with my tongue I never let my fingers stop playing with his huge cock.

His fingers trace circles on my skin as I move down.

Down his stomach and lower. Slowly, inexorably I move lower.

He lifts his hips and slides his pants up and over. His cock stands erect, straining for the stars, a beautiful specimen of desire and need.

I know it's big. I've seen it but I didn't take time to appreciate it it before. It's at least as big around as my fist. The underside is soft flesh while the top is a series of ridges slanted back into each other creating a wave leading down to his pelvis where the base ridge juts out.

Tracing the soft underside with my tongue, he cries out my name again. My heart leaps into overdrive, my pulse pounding in my ears and between my legs.

As I slide back down his shaft, I get it.

That base ridge will hit my clit.

I get it. We're compatible.

All of which means he may be big, but I can take it. I can have him.

Reaching the head of his cock I trace the ridge with my tongue.

His cock is too big for my mouth, I can only fit my lips around the head. He tangles his hand in my hair and hisses, urged on by his pleasure I press my tongue to the underside and suck.

"Olivia," he groans a warning. He can't take much more.

Climbing up along his body I pass over his cock, letting it slide along my pussy, the length parting my nether lips.

I shift until the head of his massive, pulsating cock is at my opening.

He puts his hands on my hips, stopping my downward motion.

He says something, concern in his eyes.

Biting my lip, I nod, resting my hands on his chest.

He loosens his grip but keeps his hands on my hips.

I'm on top and fully in control. I slide lower until his giant cock pierces me, the first ridge makes me groan in disbelief.

It feels so good to have him in me. Pausing, I close my eyes and enjoy it.

Slowly I go lower.

Ragnar's hands on my hips flex, his eyes close and he releases a breath in a slow hiss. His face is so beautiful.

The urge to make him lose control makes me lose my own.

I'm so wet and so ready I rock forward until he's fully inside. I'm filled beyond belief, the ridges of his cock rub me just the right way and that base ridge!

Oh my god, the ridge. It rubs right against my aching clit.

I can't help but to ride his immense cock, thrusting my hips forward and grinding against that beautiful ridge.

"Olivia," he groans.

"Yes!" I cry, both hands on his sculpted chest.

He pushes himself up until he's upright and I'm in is lap, pierced to the core. He grasps my ass in both hands and dominates my mouth with his.

I'm not in control anymore.

Ragnar thrusts his hips and devours me with tongue.

He moves us both in hard, fast motions that leave me little time to breath. My orgasm is an approaching freight train.

It hits me harder than I could have ever imagined. My entire body tenses as my pussy convulses, milking his prodigious cock. He grips my hair tightly and rapidly pistons his hips until he cries out in release, his seed spilling inside my womb.

He kisses me. Soft, gentle, caring kisses that send thrills through my body while my heart slows back to a normal pace.

Swinging my leg around, I move to lie beside him, resting my head on his shoulder, tracing the lines of his muscles with my fingertips. His spent cock lies between his legs, so impressive and I took it. All of it.

I can't help the smile that plays on my lips.

My pussy still throbs.

His cock jerks, then it slides down. Another cock rises and stands up erect and ready.

"HOLY SHIT!" I exclaim sitting up.

Ragnar looks at me with confusion on his face.

Eyes wide, I point at his... his... second cock!

"What in the hell?"

Ragnar smiles, rising onto his elbow, leaning in closer until his lips claim mine.

This guy just keeps getting better and better.

14

RAGNAR

"Guster," I say, repeating the word slowly while holding the piece of meat out to Olivia.

"Guh-sh-tah," she tries.

I repeat it a few more times until she gets it correct.

We've spent the last several days teaching each other words and mating. I am content, but Olivia is growing restless. My wings have healed and I can travel but I'm not sure I want to. We have everything we need. I've worked on the tunnel she fell into and made a passable shelter for us. We have food. I could live out my days here and be happy.

Except she's not happy and the heat is affecting her. She tries to hide it but it's in the way she moves. The color of her skin has a gray tint to it and the moisture that normally coats it isn't as much as it was.

She needs epis.

I might be able to get epis on my own but there is nothing more dangerous on Tajss than a zemlja. The risks are too high. If something went wrong it would doom Olivia.

I smoke the guster meat and store it in oiled leathers. Using the cured leather, I've made a new pack to carry the extra meat and what supplies we have left. As much as I hate it, it's time.

Olivia is walking outside our cave, a habit she started a few days ago. Every morning at dawn she walks before the suns get too high.

I pack the new bag full of meat and store the last of the healing paste then heft the two packs over my shoulder. Picking up my spear and starting out, I stop and look back.

This was good.

I don't know what lies ahead, the future is uncertain. What if she leaves me? What if something happens to her?

I've never thought like this before. Never considered life beyond the moment. The future was never my problem.

I know why.

I never had a future to look forward to. I had no hope and nothing to live for. Living was a habit, not a life.

Olivia changes that.

I have a reason to live now.

For her.

When I exit our cave she's staring out across the rolling sand dunes, arms crossing her chest, holding herself.

Walking up behind her, I wrap my arms around her, pulling her tight against me. The sweet, wonderful scent of her fills my nostrils. The curve of her, the way she fits me is perfect. She leans her head to one side and I nuzzle against her neck. She giggles as I hit a ticklish spot. Her hands rest on my arms and we stand holding each other, staring out into what I know is our future.

Tajss is beautiful but bleak with rolling dunes of sand in shades of red and white. Somewhere, out there across the empty desert, is a city. Maybe our friends made it.

The only way to find out is to go.

I think I know the way. Astarot told us the direction and I'm a hunter. I can find signs. I'll find this city, somehow.

The suns break above the horizon and the temperature takes an immediate jump up. Olivia turns in my arms and rises on her toes, offering me her lips.

Her kiss is sweet life itself.

My skin tingles at her touch and my prime penis stirs to life. She breaks the kiss, leaning back and looking at the packs on my back. Her brow furrows as she tilts her head to one side.

"It's time," I say, but she shakes her head.

Our advancement in language hasn't gone this far. Thinking about it, I try to figure out how to say what I want to tell her. Giving up I point at the horizon then nod.

She follows my arm, gazing out at the desert. She says something. A single word.

I try to sound it out, "Fff-eee-ndssss?"

The word is difficult to say, there's a hard sound in the middle that doesn't come naturally to my tongue.

She shakes her had, smiling and repeats it.

I try, several more times. "Ffrreendsss?"

Her smile outshines the suns in the sky. She nods enthusiastically.

I grab my spear from where I left it then with her at my side we start off in search of the Tribe.

Days. We travel for days without sign of our people or that we're getting any closer to the city. I remember when Tajss was alive. Airships filled the sky, ground transports zipped across the sand between major city ports. Workers went out to harvest the epis then returned with their loads.

Once that was my life, a worker. Each day I went out with my crew and we harvested then we came home. Dangerous, but that was my life. Bashir and Melchior were on my team then. We learned to work close together. We had to to survive.

Before the devastation. Before everything ended.

I knew before it started that the revolution would fail. When the war came I tried to warn the others. Only Bahsir and Melchior would listen.

Olivia touches my arm and I shake my head to clear it of unwanted memories. That was then, this is now. She is my now and my future. She is all that matters.

We travel on. It's getting harder for her, she stumbles more often. Her eyes glaze over most of the time. I keep one arm wrapped around her waist to support her. It slows us down but we have no choice.

The suns drop as we continue until shadows stretch towards us. It's not safe to travel at night so we make camp, as we have so many times before. I create a small fire, just enough to warm the meat and provide light. Our fuel supply is limited and growing smaller. If we don't find an oasis soon, there will be only cold meals and no light.

We snuggle together, chewing the tough guster meat. Her head rests against my shoulder, my arm is draped across her chest. We can barely talk but together everything feels right. Comfortable, I don't need anything else. I have her and it's perfect.

She shivers and turns into me, leaning her head back. We kiss. Our lips seeking each other, melding together.

Desire rises, fast and instant. I always want her, there's a stoked fire in my core that ignites at her slightest touch.

I kiss her deeply, exploring her mouth with my tongue. My cock is hard and ready.

Kissing my way across her cheek and down her shoulder, I make my way lower. She wriggles, shifting positions.

Her clothes slide away as I lower myself between her legs.

Her incredible scent, her delicate flower opens before me.

I drag my tongue from the bottom of her to the top, moving side to side, covering her with the moisture of my tongue while tasting her sweet juices.

She's wet so I press one finger inside and curl up, finding the spot I know she likes. Rubbing it with my finger I find the hard nub at the top of her opening and lavish it with my tongue.

Her hands curl in my hair, twisting, pulling me in closer.

"Ragnar!" she cries out, panting as she thrusts her hips up into my face.

I don't stop, building her pleasure.

My cock pounds, desperate for her but pleasing her brings its own satisfaction.

I circle her tight nub with my tongue, not touching it directly, teasing while my finger continues to work that spot deep inside.

Pulling back for a moment I touch the nub with the point of my tongue, licking up in slow motion. Dragging my tongue up then down.

She goes wild beneath me. Her hips thrust back and forth as she cries out.

Her fingers knot in my hair tighter, pulling me closer.

Wrapping an arm around her waist I hold her up.

Her body arches, muscles contracting and she's making a wordless cry that continues on as her pleasure wracks her body with its intensity.

I hold her until her body relaxes then lower her to the ground. Curling around her I let her relax, kissing her shoulder and neck.

After she's recovered, she turns in towards me, her hand slides down and grabs my cock. She strokes it until I can't hold off any longer and I explode, my pleasure spilling on the sand.

My second cock rises as she rolls over and opens herself. She's wet and ready as I slide in slowly, making sure not to hurt her.

Fully inside of her I hold then thrust. She cries out in pleasure as we find our rhythm.

We move as one, rising into each other then falling away.

The pleasure of being with her is almost more than I can stand. Full dark falls as we find ourselves in each other.

We mate for I don't know how long. Time doesn't matter. We enjoy each other until at last our climax comes as one.

Taken by storm until it passes then we fall asleep entangled in each other's arms.

I AWAKE WITH HER SNUGGLED CLOSE. SHE STIRS THEN stretches. Following suit we rise and have a quick breakfast.

Hefting the packs on my back, we take off again.

I've been guiding us by the suns and watching for signs.

So far there has been nothing but empty desert. In a few more days I'll have to hunt again.

Epis runs through my mind. The Tribe had forsaken epis, seeing it as the evil that destroyed our planet and doomed our race.

Was Lana right? Do the humans have to have it to survive?

The longer we travel the more I notice signs of exhaustion and something wrong with Olivia.

Our water supply is short so I give almost all of it to her. I don't need much but its obvious she does.

There are trace amounts of epis in the guster meat and it seems to help, but how long before it's not enough?

Supporting her with one arm as we move across the loose sand, climbing a huge dune, I worry. Time is not on my side.

"Oh!" Olivia cries out.

She is pointing ahead.

The gleaming dome is the first thing that comes into

view. Sunlight dances off it, creating rainbows in the air as it's reflected and refracted.

Olivia bounces next to me talking excitedly.

Stumbling we run together down the dune. The dome is distant but reachable in a day.

As we reach the bottom, I can barely see the top of the dome beyond the next rise. Climbing is slow, it's hard for Olivia and I all but carry her up.

We cross several more dunes, coming closer and closer. Topping yet another, something makes me stop. Closing my protective lids to see across the distance, the sight snaps into clarity.

A camp.

There are tents outside the dome and people wandering among them. Then there's Drosdan. He's so big that he stands out despite the distance. He's walking alongside what can only be the Commander.

Why are they outside the dome? The entire point was for us to move into the City. Straining to see more, to understand what is happening, I discover small figures inside the dome.

Humans. And it looks like they're armed. Standing guard.

What is going on? Olivia wavers next to me, staring into the distance, shielding her eyes with her hand. She looks up at me with confusion in her eyes. She says something. Shaking my head, I put my arm around her waist and help, pushing us forward.

The answers lie ahead.

15

OLIVIA

"*H*oly balls," I exclaim, topping another dune.

It's clear what Ragnar must have seen way back there, the Tribe have tents set up outside a domed city and there are humans inside standing guard.

"The hell is this, some kind of Game of Thrones, Wildlings versus Northerners shit?" I curse.

What I wouldn't give for some cold *Winter Is Coming* right about now. My head is pounding and my joints ache, a deep throbbing pain that doesn't stop. Every step is an effort of will and if Ragnar wasn't helping, I know I would have given up miles back.

Topping yet another dune, we reach the first of the tents. The Zmaj of the Tribe sit around small fires talking. As Ragnar and I approach, they rise to their feet. A murmur spreads before us as we walk through the growing crowd.

Zmaj call out to Ragnar and he responds.

"Olivia?" Delilah's voice cuts through the noise.

"Delilah?" I ask, looking around, trying to spot her.

Suddenly she's here, her arms wrap me in a hug and we spin. She's laughing and kissing my cheeks.

"Hi," I say, laughing too.

"Damn it, I thought I'd lost you," she says, smacking me on each cheek once more with a wet kiss before letting me go.

"You can't get rid of me that easy!"

She puts her arm around my shoulders and walks with us. Ragnar leads the way through the tents like he knows where he's going.

"I'm glad you're here," Delilah says. "This has become a total shit storm."

"What's going on?" I ask. "How long have you been here?"

"We got here two days ago."

"Two days? Why the camp? Why aren't we all in the city?"

"Yeah, about that," she says. "Turns out they pulled the welcome mat when they saw us coming over the dunes."

"What do you mean?"

"They don't want us."

"Who doesn't? I mean, that doesn't make sense! Where's Lana?"

"She's stuck outside too," Delilah says.

Ragnar's friends, Bashir and Melchior break through the crowd to embrace him. The three Zmaj talk over each other with rapid fire words I could never follow. My handful of Zmaj isn't up to the task.

"Okay, back up. Seriously, she said we'd be welcome! How can they lock us out? The City is huge! Look at that? There's plenty of room for all of us and a thousand times more!"

"I know, right?" Delilah agrees. "Yet here we are."

Ragnar grabs my arm, pulling my attention. Anger dances in his eyes, his jaw is tight, the line of his lips hard, it's obvious he's pissed. He says something, speaking too fast for me to follow. I shake my head to show I don't understand. He frowns deeper.

"Lana," he says, speaking slow, enunciating carefully.

"Right," I agree. "Where is Lana?"

"She's with Astarot and the Tribe leaders up by the dome," Delilah says, pointing towards the city.

Ragnar looks in the direction that Delilah is pointing and nods. Still gripping my arm he moves, pulling me along. Delilah follows as do Melchior and Bahsir. We form a wedge cutting through the members of the Tribe on our way towards our goal.

The tents stop thirty feet from the dome. An empty, red no-man's-land lies before us. On the other side of the dome stand men with knives and sharpened sticks, glaring. There's a protrusion that must be an airlock and in front of this stands Lana, Astarot, and the Commander. Another Zmaj stands behind the closed doorway of the lock. All of them are talking.

"You can't be serious!" Lana screams, her face flushed with anger as she throws her arms up in the air.

Astarot says something. The Zmaj behind the door shakes his head, his wings opening part way and his tail rising straight up. His scales have a red tint to them I've not seen before in any Zmaj. He leans into his words, aggressive, and Astarot is motioning with his arms then throws them up in obvious exasperation.

The Zmaj inside the dome turns his back and storms out of the airlock. Another Zmaj is just inside the dome. He tries to stop the one storming away, placing a hand on his shoulder. The angry one jerks his shoulder away, yells something and holds his hands up in a threatening way. The other Zmaj holds his hands up palms out, shaking his head, then the angry one yells again and storms off.

The remaining Zmaj looks through the dome at those camped outside, frowns, then walks away.

"DAMN IT!" Lana yells. "You egotistical douche bag!"

She shakes her fist at the retreating Zmaj inside the dome.

"What's happening?" I ask as we arrive.

Lana turns, her face purple with anger. "My city, screw you buddy! Screw you and your damn city!" she yells over her shoulder.

Ragnar looks back and forth between Lana and I, then Astarot speaks, talking in rapid fire. His words are like bullets he's speaking so fast. Confusion, the entire world is swirling around and nothing makes sense. Grabbing on to Lana with both hands, I force her attention.

"What has happened? Why is everyone out here?"

"That asshole!" she yells, glancing back over her shoulder towards the city. "Screw you Ladon!"

"Lana!" I exclaim. "Calm down. What's going on?"

"He won't let us in," Lana says, and suddenly tears are streaming down her face. "He won't let us in."

I pull her into a hug as she breaks down. Sobbing on my shoulder, I let her hide her face while she regains composure. A sick, empty feeling forms in my stomach. We're stuck outside, without shelter. I don't think any of us even considered not being allowed into the city. Surely I can't have survived all that has happened, from the wreck, to the kidnapping, to a flipping world ending sandstorm to have it all end like this?

"Welcome to hell," Delilah says from over my shoulder. "The one she calls Ladon comes down once a day to tell us to go screw ourselves."

"You're kidding me?"

"No," Lana says, standing up straight and wiping the tears from her face. "That's the short version of it but that's what's been happening."

"But... he can't!" I sputter.

"It's his city," Lana says. "Or so he claims."

"There was another Zmaj there with him," I observe.

"That's Sverre," Lana says. "He's arguing for our side but Ladon isn't budging."

"But... why?" I ask.

Lana inhales deeply then lets it out in a long, slow exhale. "Sorry," she says. "I shouldn't lose my temper like that."

She talks rapid fire in Zmaj with Ragnar, Astarot, and the Commander. Delilah and I look at each other, waiting for her to translate. The Commander taps the ground with his staff three times before turning and walking away.

"We're screwed," Delilah sighs.

"No, not yet," Lana interjects. "We can figure this out."

"Look, I just got here and I don't know what's happening or why. Can someone please explain how we got to this point?" I plead.

"Edicts," Lana says. "It's all about the damn Edicts."

"Why?" I ask. "I thought they were good, that they helped."

"Sure, those who get it, those who follow them. Ladon doesn't. They're foreign to him. He wants to establish his dominance before he'll let anyone in the city."

"What does that mean?" I ask. "Can't they have an arm wrestling match or something?"

"It's not that simple," Lana says. "He has to beat the biggest and the best."

"What the hell? Is this some macho male bullshit?"

"Of course it is!" Lana screams, turning and making a rude gesture at the city beyond the dome.

"So why doesn't he fight and we move on?" I ask.

"Because the Commander won't agree to it. He says it would be a violation of the Edicts."

Closing my eyes I try to reason my way through the morass. Conflicting views, alien concepts, none of this makes sense.

"What about them?" I ask, hooking a thumb over my shoulder at the men standing along the dome with their sticks.

Lana sighs and her face looks crestfallen. "That's a whole other issue."

"One you failed to mention before?" I ask, sarcastic yet but that's the way I'm feeling right now.

Surviving all I've been through only to reach the end of the rainbow and find out some jerk stole the promised pot of gold.

"Look, it wasn't a problem when I left. It's still not a problem."

"Well what is it, exactly, that's not a problem?" I ask.

"Those are followers of Gershom."

"What's a Gershom?" I ask.

"Not a what, a who," she corrects me. "He's an asshole. He's been spouting *Human First* nonsense since Ladon found us. He's got followers who think we shouldn't be so... friendly with the Zmaj."

"Are you kidding me? Intergalactic racism?" Delilah chimes in.

"I wish I was," she says. "I think the technical term for it is xenophobia. They hate aliens."

"Beautiful, we've been set back centuries," Delilah says.

"I know, but it's fear. They're scared for their future. They see the alien men taking the human women and they worry if there are enough of us to go around. They're also scared what will happen to our race."

"So they want the Zmaj to die out and the human race to carry on, no matter what the girl wants? Are we talking forced breeding or what?" I ask, anger rising.

"It's not that bad, well for most of them," Lana says. "They don't think it through like that. Fear isn't rational."

"Oh well that makes me feel so much better," Delilah says.

"What a mess," I observe.

"Yeah, well we have to work this out," Lana says. "There has to be a peaceful resolution."

"So the Zmaj in the City don't follow the Edicts?" I ask.

"No," Lana sighs, throwing her hands up and shaking her head. "I never heard of them until we met the Tribe."

Ragnar says something, pulling Lana's attention. The two of them talk back and forth, leaving me with time to think. The tribe has their Edicts, rules that bring them together. I assumed all Zmaj had them, but obviously that's not the case. I don't know much about the Zmaj, only bits and pieces I've picked up talking to Lana and just paying attention. Random pieces of data I've put together. That's how my mind works, it's what made me good at my job on the ship.

Being a data analyst is nothing if not seeing patterns in information. Fine but how do I use what I know? How can I make this better?

Ragnar hisses, his wings spread and his tail goes still. He leans forward, aggressive, but Lana holds her ground, raising her voice.

"What?" I ask, stepping closer to Ragnar and putting my hand over his balled fist.

"He's an idiot!" Lana yells, then says something in Zmaj.

Ragnar hisses low, dangerous, and Astarot steps up beside her. Great, now these two will get into a fight. Just what we needed.

"Stop!" I yell, pulling down on Ragnar's arm.

Its ineffectual, he's stronger than I am and I know I won't move him if he doesn't allow me to but he lowers his fist, turning his head until our eyes meet. He says something I wish I understood. If only I could talk to him I know I could make things better.

Lana looks back and forth between the two of us, her eyes wide and her mouth hanging open. She knows what he said but isn't saying it out loud. Astarot says something but Ragnar doesn't take his eyes off of mine.

"Olivia," Lana says.

"What?" I ask, my hand on Ragnar's fist, my eyes locked with his.

"So… do you know…" Lana says, trailing off.

"Know what Lana?"

"How he, uhm, feels about you?"

"Yep, I think I do. Why?"

"Okay," Lana says. "Do you know… what that means?"

"Lana, tell me what he said. Enough beating around the bush."

"He said he'll take the city, for you, alone if he has to."

My heart melts. Why does a professed act of violence have this effect on me? I'm not even going to pretend to understand. He would do that for me. Because I'm that important to him. More important than anything else in the world.

Placing my hand on his cheek, I rise on my toes until our lips meet. He wraps his arms around me, lifting my off my feet. We kiss, in front of everyone, and I don't care. Let them stare. Let them see he chose me. I'm his, the only one he wants.

Lana clears her throat loud enough to cut into the moment. I break the kiss with great reluctance and Ragnar puts me back on my feet.

"So you're… okay with this?" Lana asks.

"How could I not be?"

"Okay, good," she says.

She says something to Astarot who smiles then steps forward and takes Ragnar's hand. He pulls Ragnar into an embrace, patting his back with his closed fist. The two Zmaj break apart and then that moment is over.

"Has anyone talked to the Zmaj inside about the Edicts?" I ask.

"Ladon isn't listening," Lana says.

"Why is it all up to Ladon?"

"The City is, technically, his," Lana says. "No one has challenged him on that. It's never been necessary before."

"But there are other Zmaj living in there with him."

"Yes, but they came one or two at a time. He could control them and establish himself as the dominant one," Lana answers. "This is more threatening."

Looking out across the tents dotting the desert it makes sense, in a primal, alpha male sort of way.

The only question is, how do we get past it?

A commotion on the inside of the city dome pulls my attention. The humans standing in a line along the dome have turned, too. Two Zmaj approach the airlock. It's the same two I saw before.

The one in the lead punches at the box next to the airlock then they enter. It swooshes as it shuts.

I'm holding my breath, waiting to see what happens next.

The crowd on our side murmurs and shifts as the Commander makes his way back.

Tension is so thick I could cut it with a knife. The oppressive heat beating down is making me light-headed. Maybe it's stress.

I have no idea what's about to happen, this could go wrong in an instant. I gasp a quick breath as the outer airlock door hisses, letting out the pent up air.

The Zmaj in the lead steps out, aggressive and angry looking.

16

RAGNAR

*P*ushing Olivia gently behind me as I turn towards the dome, I'm ready.

The ancient airlock opens and two Zmaj come out. The one in the lead is aggressive, his anger showing in the color of his scales. He moves forward, a storm of emotion. His balled fists, tight jaw, stiff tail all give away his feelings.

He's close to losing control to the bijass. If he does, this will go bad quickly.

Visidion steps out of the crowd, his second, Drosdan, right behind.

"I didn't ask you here," the new Zmaj says, coming to a stop before the Commander.

"No," Visidion agrees. "You did not."

"Why do you camp here? You are not welcome!"

"We come in peace. Together we are stronger," the Commander answers, remaining calm.

The anger pulsing off of the new Zmaj calls to my bijass. That primal part of me surges in response to his threatening posture and words. Crying out to establish dominance.

"One, I am myself. Two, together we are stronger. Three,

survival of the group matters," the Commander says, leaning on his staff as he recites the Edicts.

Drosdan hisses in agreement, or he's just being a general ass, I'm not sure. Drosdan leans towards the latter, depending on his size and strength to carry him through.

"What are you talking about?" the new Zmaj demands.

"As I've said, Ladon, we should talk. Violence is unnecessary here," the second Zmaj says, holding his hands out palms up.

"They came to my city," the one called Ladon snaps over his shoulder. "Uninvited!"

"I wasn't invited when I arrived either," the second says. "Yet you welcomed me. We have space, let us work this out."

"My space," Ladon snaps. "Shut up Sverre. This is no time for your diplomacy."

"Rosalind asked that I be here," Sverre says.

"This is not her city either!" Ladon retorts.

"Ladon," the Commander says. "We intend no threat to your domain."

"Yet you are here," Ladon says, leaning into his words..

"Yes, we are," the Commander nods.

"You're not welcome, I do not want you here," Ladon says.

Drosdan hisses and steps up beside the Commander. Ladon shifts his focus to the big Zmaj.

As if watching it happen in slow motion, I can see where this will end.

"Your size doesn't intimidate me," Ladon hisses, his scales flushing with a red tint.

"Let's see," Drosdan answers, his massive fists coming up.

"Drosdan, stop," I interject. "Edicts, together are stronger."

Drosdan glares before nodding and lowering his hands. It's obvious he's struggling with his own bijass. Ladon shifts his glare from Drosdan back to the Commander.

Olivia rests her hand on my back, just below my wings. Glancing over my shoulder at her, she smiles reassuringly.

She is all that matters. I have to make this work for her.

"We have much to discuss," the Commander says.

"There is nothing to discuss, I don't want you here," Ladon repeats.

"Ladon," Sverre cautions.

The door to the city whooshes and everyone turns to look.

Two women are in the airlock about to walk out, unexpected enough, but what they carry in their arms changes everything.

Olivia gasps, stepping next to me.

Blinking I look again, then again.

Babies.

They're carrying babies.

With wings.

And Scales.

The babies have wings and scales yet they aren't fully Zmaj.

They're carried by two human females.

One baby is larger, the female carrying it has a long mane that comes past her shoulders, pale skin, and full red lips. The baby on her hip is several months old. It has to be. It's been so long since I've seen a child that I can't really tell.

The baby smiles, laughing, tiny, membranous wings spread then close. A tiny tail shifts back and forth excitedly. Its small, perfect little hands grip the blouse of the female tight. It has dark hair and its scales are a light yellow-tan color.

"Papa," the baby says.

The other baby is every bit as miraculous. The female carrying it is shorter in stature, with golden skin and her eyes have an interesting tilt. Different from the other human females. Her child is smaller, obviously not as old yet. Its hair is sparser and its scales have a darker tint with a stronger blue cast.

Ladon turns when the first baby speaks and everything changes.

Olivia says something in a soft exhale. I may not understand her words but I share the sentiment, as does everyone here.

"Those are..." I say.

Ladon turns to look at me, frowning, anger flashing in his eyes.

"What?" he asks, moving his body to block the view of the child.

Shaking my head, I struggle to find words that won't come out wrong.

"Yours?" I ask, giving up on finding better words.

"Yes," Ladon answers, leaning aggressively.

"That means..." Turning, I look at Olivia and a new, brighter future than I ever dared hope for shines. I hadn't considered the possibility that maybe we could...

Olivia, her hand on my shoulder, gasps as the woman with the larger baby says something in their human tongue. One drop of the moisture rolls down my treasure's cheek and I wipe it away.

She throws her arms around me and I take her in my embrace.

A future.

"So what are you boys all doing out here in the heat?" the female with the older baby asks in perfect Zmaj.

She stands next to Ladon, and it's more than obvious that they belong to one another. No Zmaj could miss the connection, the claim he has on her.

"We are discussing the terms of our entrance to your fair city," the Commander says, diplomatic as ever.

"And all these girls are just out here melting while they wait?" the other female asks, also in perfect Zmaj.

The Commander says nothing. Ladon looks away.

"Ladon, honey," the first female says.

"No," Ladon replies, not meeting her eyes.

She moves over to him, placing a hand on his chest. The baby on her hips holds its arms up towards him.

"Papa," the baby says, its voice high and almost squeaking.

Ladon takes the child, lifting it up, then kisses it on each cheek before holding it close to his chest.

"Ladon," the female says again. "Let us bring the women inside."

She puts a hand on his chest next to the baby. They look into each other's eyes.

"We do not have enough epis for them," he says, making a sweeping motion with his arm.

"We'll be fine," she assures him.

"Our supplies are low," he says.

"They brought their own," she answers.

He frowns and it's obvious he wants to argue more, but it's also just as obvious that she will win.

"Fine," he says at last. "The females only."

She rises on her toes and kisses him. Deep and passionate. When they part, she takes the baby.

"Come to mommy, Illadon," she says.

The baby coos and laughs, switching from his father to his mother.

Everyone is watching. No one dares speak.

Lana walks over and speaks with the two women holding the babies. The three of them embrace each other and it's obvious they are all friends. Olivia slides an arm around my waist and I rest mine across her shoulders.

Our two species can have babies.

Astarot and I lock eyes across the heads of the females. He

smiles. He knew this was possible. He nods as if understanding what I'm thinking.

The females huddle together and talk. When they're finished the one talking with Ladon whistles, getting everyone's attention.

"All right boys," she says. "You will all stay out here and work our your differences. Meanwhile, the women are all coming inside with us."

Cold shock hits me. No.

Instinctively I tighten my grip around Olivia. She places a hand on my chest and I look down, feeling selfish at seeing her terrible condition. The heat is too much for her, she needs the better air inside the city. She needs epis.

She says something. Her fingers trail a hot line across my cheek, down across my neck.

I close my eyes, bracing myself for what I know I must do.

I let her go.

The hardest single thing I've ever done in my life.

She lingers against me then steps away, staring over her shoulder as she walks over to the women with the babies.

More females come out of the camp until they are all huddled together. As a group they're led to the airlock and through. Olivia is among the last, then they are all inside the dome.

Inside the city. Blocked off from me.

As the group heads into the city, she looks over her shoulder until we can't see each other any longer.

It feels as if a part of me is walking away, leaving an empty void where she should be.

17

OLIVIA

"This is nice," Delilah says.

"Yeah, it's not bad," Calista says, shifting the baby from one hip to the other. "We're working on it."

It's strange to be walking down a ruined city street like this. The ship was meant to feel like a city, but you still knew you were in an enclosed area surrounded by empty space.

Here is different. The sidewalks are some kind of manufactured stone where the ship was steel covered with a rubber. The buildings are in a bad state of repair. There are a lot of broken windows and dirt and grime. Topping it all off, red sand dusts everything. Everything has a reddish-yellow cast to it thanks to the dome. Looking up, it is so far above, arcing over the entire city. It filters the light of the dual suns, dimming it and also reducing the heat.

The temperatures aren't as hot inside as it is outside but it's not cool and comfortable either.

One of the new girls drops back through the group to walk next to me. The baby on her hip coos and waves with the most adorable smile I've ever seen. I wiggle my fingers and he giggles. Him. Well I assume it's a him.

He opens his tiny, membranous wings that are so thin the light shines through and flaps them, his little tail shifting side to side in obvious excitement.

"Hi," the new girl says. "I'm Calista, this is Illadon."

"Hi," I say.

"So," Calista says. "What's his name?"

"I'm sorry?" I ask, taken by surprise with her blunt question.

Calista smiles, hefts the baby up higher on her waist, then repeats the question.

"Ragnar," I say, flushing.

Calista nods, pursing her lips and looking thoughtful.

"Illadon, what a cute name," I say.

"Thanks, it's a bit of an homage, blending his father's name with an old earth game."

"Oh," I say.

"Jolie named her little one Rverre," Calista adds, nodding up at the other baby ahead of us.

"River?" I ask.

"Exactly," Calista says. "Jolie is firmly in the Doctor Who camp. She thought it was a clever way to keep the naming tradition I started going. Rverre is a combination of River Song and Sverre. Personally, I'm in the Star Trek camp."

"The... camp?" I ask, confused.

"You all didn't divide? Not enough geeks in your part of the ship?" she asks, laughing.

"Well, I'm a data nerd, I guess."

"You guess?" Calista says, her smile makes it clear she's joking with me.

I shrug and laugh, feeling lost and wishing with all my heart that Ragnar was at my side.

"So how long have you and Ragnar been an item?" she asks.

"An item?" I play dumb, trying to buy time to figure out an answer.

What do I say? I don't know when it happened. Are we an item? We can't even talk to each other. What does that say about me as a person that I'm sleeping with a guy I can't even talk to? Is it more than just an ongoing one night stand? My heart says it is. I think his does to. No, I know his does. How do I explain that to, well, anyone?

"I get it," Calista says, dropping her voice so that only I can hear her when she notices some of the girls ahead glancing over their shoulders.

"Do you?"

"Yeah," she says. "I was… first."

"What do you mean, first?"

"Ladon found me after we crashed," she says. "I brought him to the others but only after we had… well, you know."

Nodding my understanding, a bond forms. First. We have that in common at least.

"Yeah," I agree. "Me too, I guess. No one else anyway has… well as far as I know."

Calista nods and smiles. "So tell me all about it. How are there so many Zmaj together out there? That's unbelievable! When word came in there was an army of Zmaj approaching the dome we were freaking out."

"How come?" I ask.

"Zmaj don't get along, not since the extinction event they call the Devastation."

Frowning I think about that. I've not seen anything like that. They are primal, barbaric maybe, but the Tribe all get along well enough.

"I've not seen that in the Tribe," I say.

"The Tribe?" she asks.

"Yeah, that's what they call themselves, according to Lana," I say.

"Hmm."

"I can't talk to them though," I say. "How did you learn their language? Can you help me?"

"Sure," Calista says. "It's easier than you might think. Didn't Lana tell you?"

"No, I haven't thought to talk to her about it."

I'm trying to take in as much of the city as I can while we walk.There are no short buildings, everything looks like it's at least twenty decks high or more.

"So how much do you know about Zmaj?" Calista asks, probing for something but I'm not sure what.

"Enough, I guess," I shrug.

"Have you two..." she trails off, flushing a deep red as she continues. "Have you seen him naked?"

"Yeah," I say, my cheeks burning just as hot.

"Okay, good," Calista says. "That can be a shocker."

"Oh my god, yes!" I agree and Calista laughs.

"You know Zmaj mate for life?" she asks.

"They do?"

"Yes, if he's chosen you, you're his treasure. It's a much deeper bond than anything you'll have experienced before."

Thinking back on my limited, almost non-existent, 'experience' I don't know that I'd know the difference but I can't stop myself from smiling at memories of the way he touches me, the way he looks at me. Treasure is a good word. I feel treasured when I'm with him. Like I'm the most important thing in his universe.

"I think I get it."

"Good," she says.

"Scum," someone says loudly from ahead of us.

There are three, scraggly looking men and a woman walking in a group away from us across the street.

"Eat dick," one of the other girls yells.

One of the men stops and turns towards her, but the

other three grab him by his shoulders and pull him away. They glare at us without another word, not breaking their gaze until they turn the corner out of sight.

"What was that?" I ask.

"Gershom supporters," Calista sighs.

"I heard something about him outside," I say.

"Yeah, sorry. Even lost on a desert planet, some people are just assholes."

"Are there a lot of them?"

"No, maybe, it's hard to tell," she says. "I think many people are just afraid. He's fantastic at playing on that."

"I see."

"Yeah, well don't worry about those jerks."

"Okay," I agree, doing my best to put them out of my mind.

"I want to know more about you all," Calista says. "None of us could believe it when we found out another section of the ship survived the crash! Tell me all about it. I want to know everything."

"Well, everything is a lot." The sad loss of our part of the ship isn't really a story that's fun to tell.

"You got something better to do?" she asks, grinning.

Her smile is infectious so I launch into my story, telling her about surviving the pirate attack on our ship, then crashing on the planet. Learning to survive here on our own, getting taken by the Zmaj, then coming to terms with the loss of friends and family when we went back.

"So you've had run-ins with the pirates here?" I ask.

"They haven't tried anything at the city but yes," she says. "They've been spotted and dealt with by some of us out on expeditions. Amara dealt with a lot of them."

"Which one is Amara," I ask, looking at the group of women just ahead.

"She's not with us," Calista smiles. "She's in her final quarter."

"Her final quarter?"

"Uhm, yeah. Well if you conceive, there's a few things we've figured out you should know."

"Like?"

"Zmaj babies are big. They take longer to gestate than the normal baby cycle."

"How bad is it?" I ask, my throat dry and tight.

"Just an extra three or four months…" she trails off.

"Okay?"

"But it requires bed rest. Our bodies aren't designed to carry a baby that long."

"Oh," I say, nerves tingling along my arms and legs with a restlessness which makes me feel out of sorts.

"It's not bad," she says, shifting Illadon who coos and calls out, reaching his perfect, tiny little hands towards me. "And the result is absolutely worth it."

She kisses Illadon's head, smiling. The cold ball of ice in my stomach melts seeing the result of a pregnancy. I hold out my finger to him and Illadon grabs onto it with a surprisingly strong grip. He pulls my finger to his mouth and chews.

"I think he's teething," I observe.

"Yes, all his hand-crafted toys are now chew things," Calista says. "Oh, we're here."

We walk into a large, open area. A fountain with a statue of a Zmaj dominates the center. There is no water in it as far as I can tell and the statue has chips and cracks. The group is heading towards a building on the far side of the square that has large, intact front windows.

Jolie, holding her baby on her hip, holds the door open, ushering all of us inside. Calista and I are the last to enter.

"You two getting along?" Jolie asks.

"She's sweet," Calista says, causing a burning flush to race across my cheeks.

"Thank you," I squeak. "I'm glad to get to know you."

"Don't let her fool you," Jolie says. "Calista can be totally ruthless."

"Look who's talking," Calista retorts, laughing.

The friendship and connection these two share is deep and obvious.

"Your baby is Rverre?" I ask, looking at the small child on her hip.

There's a delicateness to the baby's features that Illadon doesn't have. The wings are different looking, more membranous maybe? The tail is thinner and longer despite it being smaller overall.

"Yes!" Jolie says, beaming with excitement. "Her name is Rverre. She's growing like a weed too."

Jolie hefts the baby up and down on her hip making her giggle loudly. The baby has brilliant green eyes that sparkle with joy and a toothless smile that makes her cheeks stick out.

"Pfff, should have named her Jadzia," Calista huffs.

"Ugh, like I'd ever name her after a Star Trek character," Jolie says, shaking her head.

"I'm telling you Olivia, some people have no taste," Calista says, struggling to keep a straight face.

"I know, right? How can you not love Doctor Who?" Jolie insists.

"Truly a dilemma," I observe, trying to tread my way through the obvious minefield.

"A diplomat," Jolie observes. "Well played."

The three of us laugh together as we enter the building.

Inside the air is cooler than outside, not a lot, it's not air conditioner but it's better. We're in a large lobby area that looks like it once served as a reception. Now it seems like some sort of communal gathering area.

"Bunch of fucking bullshit," someone grouses.

Half of the room has seats, small tables, and a bed that dominates the space. On that bed is another woman with a belly that is so swollen I wonder she doesn't explode right there. She has a strong jaw and sharp nose. Her short, dark hair is standing on end and her eyes look exhausted. The other girls have taken up seats and are working on various tasks. The woman in the bed glares at Calista from across the room.

"How much longer?" she asks.

"Amara, we've talked about this," Calista sighs. "There's no way of really knowing."

"Sure, you've talked, I've listened, nothing has changed. I'm telling you Calista, this sucks."

"Where's Shidan?" Jolie asks.

"Ugh," Amara groans. "I sent him to get me food, cause you know, I'm not big enough!"

"You're beautiful," Calista says.

"Sure," she says. "If you like your women big enough to hide from a nuclear assault behind."

Calista laughs as she walks over to the bedside. "Amara, this is Olivia," she says, pointing. "She has a... special friend too."

Amara looks over at me and smiles, it's faint but genuine.

"Hey," she says. "Don't let him knock you up. This is all a bunch of bullshit."

"Amara!" Jolie says.

Calista and Jolie place their babies on the floor where they immediately become the center of attention. The two children seem most interested in each other while all the girls in the place ooh and ahh.

"What?" Amara asks. "This sucks."

"I'm sorry you're having a rough time of it," I try, unsure what else to say.

Amara shrugs.

A pale girl with white-blond hair checks her forehead and cheeks then leans in and looks into her eyes. Amara pushes her away.

"Nothing's changed," she grouses. "I'm fine."

"I know," she says, ignoring Amara. "Now let me do my job."

"See what I mean?" Amara asks, looking at me past the girl.

"Amara, do you have to be so mean?"

"Yes, Mei, I do," Amara grumps. "This sucks."

"I didn't mind it," Jolie tosses in.

"You liked being waited on," Amara says. "I want to get up and work!"

"Have you figured out how that panel we brought you works?" Jolie asks.

"No," Amara says, throwing her hands up. "I can barely hold the stupid thing up around the giant mound that is my stomach."

"It's not your stomach, that's the baby," Calista says.

"In my stomach," Amara comes back.

"No, in your uterus," Mei says, taking Amara's wrist between her thumb and fingers, closing her eyes and moving her lips as she counts.

"Same difference," Amara says.

"Okay, your pulse is fine, eyes look fine, you're good for another day," Mei says.

"Yay, another day of sitting here waiting."

"Yup," Calista says, cheerfully.

Amara rolls her eyes.

"What are you working on?" Delilah asks, her interest in engineering stuff peaked.

Jolie takes me by the arm, leading me away from Amara's bed. Calista comes to join us while Amara and Delilah talk and get to know each other. Amara seems to cheer up talking to Delilah, so that's good. Maybe they have something in common.

"Come with us," Calista whispers.

They lead the way out of the room quickly and quietly. I go along with them, uncertain what we're doing or where we're going. Calista leads us further into the building and as we walk through yet another door, there are floor to ceiling panels off to one side with data running up and down them. Screens, data, information, it calls to my heart of hearts. This is what I am, a data analyst. It doesn't matter what the data is, I love studying it, finding patterns. It makes me happy. There are also cubicles made of clear glass, most of them look shattered and ruined but one has a small table and a screen with rolling information.

"We've gotten this working at least," Jolie says.

"You're going to love this," Calista adds.

"What are we doing?" I ask, butterflies dancing in my stomach.

"Teaching you to speak Zmaj," Jolie grins.

"Seriously?"

"You bet," Calista says, grinning from ear to ear.

In moments I'm standing inside one booth looking at the screen. Calista reaches around me and taps on the small counter. It lights up and symbols dance across it.

"What's this going to do?"

"Just wait for it," she says.

I step back, my nerves suddenly getting the best of me.

"Look, I'm good, I'll just..."

"Olivia," Jolie says. "You don't have to if you don't want to, of course, but trust us. It's a machine that will put the Zmaj language into your head in seconds. All of it, you'll speak it fluently."

I'd be able to talk with Ragnar. Actually talk to him.

"All right, I'm in," I say, stepping back in to where they placed me before.

Calista taps the counter again, hitting the arcane symbols. A blue light flashes and shines in my eyes.

"Good!" Jolie says.

"What do you mean, good?" I ask. "It didn't do anything."

Jolie and Calista exchange a knowing smile.

"You sure about that?" Jolie asks.

"I am, nothing happened," I reply. "What?"

"You're speaking Zmaj," Calista says and they both laugh.

"I am?" I ask, trying to listen to myself.

They nod and laugh, wiping tears away from their eyes.

Footsteps running on the hard floor jerks our attention away from each other.

I follow behind as they run back towards the main gathering room we just left.

A tall, fair skinned woman stands struggling for breath just inside the door. "They did it," she pants. "Can't believe it. They did it. Come quick."

"Did what Inga?" Calista asks, rushing to the woman's side.

"Gershom's people," Inga pants. "They destroyed the airlock."

"Son of a bitch," Amara exclaims from her bed.

A cold, sick feeling grips my stomach. If they destroyed the airlock, how will I get back to Ragnar?

18

RAGNAR

I watch Olivia for as long as I can see her. Only when she turns a corner and I lose sight of her, do I return my attention to the newcomers.

"The city is mine," Ladon is saying, yet again.

It's like he's on repeat, holding to that single train of thought. He doesn't seem to be in the claws of his bijass, though I can feel its pull.

"We are not challenging that," Visidion says.

"Good, then leave," Ladon says.

"Ladon," the one called Sverre says.

"Ladon, the Tribe is friendly. There's no call to be this way," Astarot says. "They took Lana and I in and welcomed us. How can we do any less?"

"We?" Ladon hisses, turning his attention to Astarot. "I brought you others in but it's still my city. This many Zmaj? No. It's mine. My territory, my city. I will not cede control."

"This is an enormous city, a big territory," the Commander says. "Perhaps we could share?"

"Why would I share what is mine?" Ladon says, stubbornly digging his heels in to his single-minded argument.

"Together we are stronger," Visidion insists.

"So you say," Ladon answers. "Yet I have the City."

"Once, thousands of Zmaj lived here. Worked here. Raised families and died here. What does it gain you to be alone?" our Commander asks.

"Mine. What else matters," Ladon hisses, leaning in aggressively.

Drosdan steps forward, inserting himself between the Commander and Ladon. Our Second in command towers over Ladon and is at least as twice as wide across the chest and shoulders.

Ladon looks up, craning his neck back. His wings unfold and flutter, his tail stands out straight. As fast as lightning striking, his fist shoots out, slamming into Drosdan's face with enough force it reverberates in my bones. Drosdan barely turns his face. One massive hand goes to his jaw, rubs, then he leans back and it's all happening in slow motion. Drosdan brings both his hands down on Ladon's shoulders with crushing force. Ladon bows under the weight, his knees buckling part way but he holds himself upright. An impressive feat of strength. Drosdan hisses, his wings spread wide, his tail standing up. Ladon punches, rapid fire hits into Drosdan's stomach. It's enough to break Drosdan's grip as he stumbles backwards.

Ladon doesn't let up, pushing his advantage as Drosdan falls back.

Drosdan's wings spread as he roars with rage. The people circled around the fight take a step back. Drosdan's bijass is strong, a siren call to all of us to give in to our own primal nature.

Ladon hisses but doesn't slow his advance. Crouching low, he weaves back and forth, closing with Drosdan who stands ready with his arms spread wide. The two circle each other. The smaller Zmaj feints in and out, probing for an opening, but Drosdan moves to block each assault.

Despite his size, Drosdan is quick.

"Ragnar!" the Commander calls. He motions towards the fight and I know what he wants.

A deep, primal part of me says to stay out of it. Let the two of them fight it out. See who wins then establish myself as that one's better.

Closing my eyes I take a deep breath.

No.

The Edicts.

I am myself.

I am not the primal monster inside.

The bijass is a darkness reaching, gripping, trying to pull me down.

I struggle to control it, to remain myself.

Hands tighten into fists, tail shifting, I hiss as the urges rise and fall.

Slipping. I'm slipping.

Olivia.

Her beautiful, perfect face fills my mind's eye. Her smile. Her soft touch.

The rage recedes.

I am myself.

Opening my eyes once more. I look anew. Together we are stronger. The Commander is right, this has to stop.

Ladon and Drosdan circle. Ladon tenses, he's about to attack.

Leaping into the air I spread my wings and glide to land between the two males. "Enough!" I yell, standing with a hand facing each.

Both of them hiss and for an instant I'm the focus of their primal rage.

The moment stretches, walking a razor's edge, will they attack me or control themselves?

No matter, I draw strength from Olivia.

"Think of your child," I say, looking at Ladon.

His hands drop as my words cut through the bijass and reach to the male beyond the primal urges.

Drosdan steps forward, hissing, and I turn.

"Move," Drosdan insists.

"No," I say, standing my ground as I stare into the larger male's eyes.

"Kill him," Drosdan says, his primal rage limiting his vocabulary.

"No," I say. "Together we are stronger."

Drosdan frowns, something flickers in his eyes. Placing a hand on his chest, I wait for him to calm. He looks down, staring at my hand, then back up to meet my eyes. One massive fist rises, cocking back, and I'm sure he's about to hit me. If he does, I don't know that I can maintain myself. Everything rides on Drosdan gaining control of his bijass.

"I am myself," Drosdan says, dropping his arm to his side.

"Survival of the group matters," Drosdan and I say as one.

Drosdan nods, taking my forearm and I grasp his, then the Second returns to stand behind the Commander.

Turning back to Ladon I hold my arm out.

Ladon stares at it then at me. No one speaks, the crowd around us waiting with bated breath.

Ladon takes my offer, we clasp forearm to forearm. The crowd breathes a collective sigh of relief.

Sverre moves up to stand beside Ladon.

"As I was saying," the Commander says, taking up his conversation as if nothing happened. "Once thousands of Zmaj lived here. Can we not work out an agreement to share some of your space?"

Ladon's jaw tightens. Sverre watches closely as do I. The claim to the city is his, he'll have final say in any negotiation unless we want to take it from him. That is not a path the Commander will walk.

"I will consider this," Ladon says.

"That is all we can ask," the Commander says. "Would you join us for water?"

My stomach tenses waiting for his answer. The tension in the air rises because what he says next will decide the future and everyone close knows it.

"Yes," Ladon says, after a quick glance over his shoulder at Sverre.

The Commander smiles then motions with his staff. Someone offers two skins. Visidion and Ladon each take one.

"Water," the Commander says, holding his towards Ladon.

"Water," Ladon agrees.

They each take a drink then hand the skins back.

"There is much to discuss," the Commander says. "Perhaps we can sit with the Council of Elders?"

"You have a Council of Elders?" Sverre asks.

"We do," the Commander says. "Led by my father, Kalessin."

Sverre does a double-take. "Kalessin?"

"Yes," Visidion says.

I'm losing interest in the conversation. My thoughts are turning to my brother, Ryuth. I haven't looked in on him. Did they get him through the storm okay?

Ryuth, I thought he was dead for years. When the pirates attacked the Tribe in our valley, they used him as a berserker to lead their assault. We subdued him but he has given himself over to his bijass. I need time to work with him, to coax him back to sanity.

"I see," Sverre says, obviously saying less than he means.

"I will sit with them," Ladon says. "The humans have a Council too, but the final decision about the City remains mine."

"Of course," the Commander agrees. "We must decide how we can best work together. Together we are stronger."

"I've heard your people say that often," Ladon says. "What does this mean?"

"The Edicts, as laid down by my Father," the Commander says. "It was his vision of what would come that led him into the wilds. The Edicts keep us strong, bring us together, allow us to work together."

"That is how there are so many of you?" Ladon asks, motioning towards the tents.

"Yes," the Commander answers. "It is how we work together."

Ladon shakes his head and opens his mouth to speak when something happens.

There is a loud crash then a harsh, buzzing noise.

Turning towards the sound, sparks are flying behind the dome. A human male is dancing and screaming, his clothes smoking as he bounds from foot to foot.

A small group of males, those who lined the inside of the dome with their sticks, rush towards him. One of them tackles the man and rolls across the ground with him.

Another group comes rushing from somewhere deeper in the city.

"No," Sverre yells.

Sverre and Ladon run towards the dome. I run with them. I'm not sure what just happened but the sick pit that forms in my stomach tells me it's not good.

The human males inside stand in a group. The two that were rolling on the ground stand up. The one whose clothing was smoking pats at burnt holes that still have drifts of smoke curling off them. One of them steps forward and points at us Zmaj gathered by the airlock door. He has a malicious grin on his face.

19

OLIVIA

*M*y heart races in my chest and I'm breathing heavy, ragged gasps, struggling to keep up with the group running through the city. I'm in no shape for this.

Through a sheer act of will I force myself to keep moving. The stitch in my side comes in so hard I bite my lower lip to avoid crying out. I don't think I'm even hydrated enough to sweat.

This isn't the way it's supposed to be. We made it, damn it. How can everything go so damn wrong!

I'm trailing behind. Can't keep up. Stupid, stupid body.

My thighs burn, stars dance in my vision, still I push forward. No stopping. Can't stop, have to reach him. Have to find a way.

Fire. My lungs are on fire. Every inhale sears.

No more. I can't make another step.

I do. Somehow. One more. Another. Can't look ahead. Can't stop. One foot after another. Keep going.

The dome sparkles ahead as we round a corner. There are two groups of people shouting at each other. Striding out between them in a brilliant white outfit strides a tall woman. Long, dark hair flows down past her shoulders. She's imperious and commanding, her presence demands respect.

Though I've never seen her in person, I recognize her. The Lady General Rosalind. Commander of the ship's fighting force. The stories about her are wild and varied, from tales of kindness to ones of unbelievably cold cruelty.

Rosalind steps between the two groups and the shouting stops as she looks from one to the other. The group of women I'm with move closer but stand apart to one side. Rosalind looks over her shoulder at us before turning her attention to the door.

"What happened here?" she asks.

"That son of a bitch Petras smashed the door lock!" a scruffy looking man standing at the front of one group yells, pointing at someone in the other group.

Rosalind glances at the scruffy man. It's only a glance but he shrinks before it. I mean, damn, she doesn't even have to speak.

"Your ladyship," the man adds, not meeting her eyes. "I mean to say... Petras over there, he smashed the door, you see."

Rosalind turns her attention to the pointed out man. The one she's looking at has black, burnt looking holes throughout his clothing and singed hair.

"Petras?" Rosalind asks.

"Yeah?" Petras replies, not meeting her eyes.

"Well?"

"Yeah, I did it," he says.

Rosalind stares, waiting.

"They deserved it. We don't need no more of them in here," Petras adds.

"You made this decision on your own?" Rosalind asks, one perfect eyebrow arching up.

"What are you implying Rosalind?" a new voice asks.

An average sized man steps through the group that Petras is with. He has gray at the temples of his dark hair, a deeply lined, tan face and big hands. He's dressed in a three piece suit despite the heat and looks almost as impeccable as Rosalind, but not quite.

"I'm not implying anything Gershom," Rosalind says. "I'm inquiring."

"Is this man on trial?" Gershom asks. "Have we fallen so far from our roots we now enforce vigilante justice?"

"An investigation Gershom. Asking questions doesn't violate anyone's rights."

"Isn't it? He's being questioned without representation."

"He admitted he did it," Rosalind counters. "The only question now is why."

I'm still trying to catch my breath but the burning stitch in my side is easing up at least.

"Is that true Petras? Did you do this?" Gershom asks, turning to look at him.

"Yeah, yes sir," Petras says, his eyes darting to Gershom then away, then back again.

He's shifty looking. Untrustworthy.

"I see," Gershom says. "Well that is a most unfortunate decision."

"We need to know why he did it," Rosalind interjects.

"We do," Gershom says, turning to look at the man. "Petras why did you do this heinous act?"

"Huh?" Petras says, looking up in his confusion. "Haynes?"

Gershom smiles, placing a hand on Petras' shoulder.

"Terrible thing," Gershom says, explaining the word.

"Oh, well, because we don't need no more of their kind in here. You ought to know," he says, smiling with what I can only describe as relief.

"I see," Gershom says. "Well, there you go Rosalind. That is why he did it."

"Who put him up to it?" she demands.

"Put him up to it?" Gershom asks. The grin on his face tells me all I need to know. Listening to Gershom makes me feel slimy. Gross. I don't trust a thing he says.

Something flashes outside the dome, catching my attention. When I look, Ragnar is standing on the other side and my heart leaps into my throat. I stumble forward a step before I realize it.

He's worried about me. I smile trying to reassure him.

"Yes Gershom," Rosalind says, her voice cutting. "Put him up to it. Where did he get such an idea?"

"Petras?" Gershom asks, turning to face the man.

"I don't guess I understand the question. I wasn't put up to it, I did it because its the right thing. We don't need no more cross-breeding going on," he says, scratching his head.

"And there you go," Gershom says, a smile that goes from ear to ear spread across his face.

Rosalind stares with pursed lips. A murmur starts in the crowd behind her as the tension rises. A tingling sensation races across my skin as I realize that this moment could go either way. Depending on what she says and does, this will resolve peacefully or devolve into something like a riot.

Rosalind senses it too. She nods to Gershom.

"Very well," she says. "Take Petras into custody. We need to arrange a trial of his peers."

"Of course," Gershom says.

He holds up a hand and circles one finger in the air. Two men behind him move over and take Petras by either arm then lead him away.

"But I didn't do nothing wrong!" Petras cries over his shoulder.

No one responds.

"All right everyone," Rosalind says. "You should all have jobs you're supposed to be doing, so let's get to it. Anyone that knows something about electronics, come help me with this door. Amara's out and I don't have another engineer."

"I can help," Delilah says, stepping forward from the group.

"Who are you?" Rosalind asks.

"Delilah."

"You're from the other part of the ship, right?" Rosalind asks.

Oh my god, I try not to fan-girl but she really is amazing. How did she know that already?

"Yeah," Delilah says.

"I'll try to help, too" I add.

I'm not an engineer but I'm good at seeing patterns, it might help.

"And you are?" Rosalind asks.

Butterflies dance in my stomach when she looks at me like I'm being weighed and judged.

"I'm Olivia."

"Good, you two get to it," Rosalind says.

Delilah grins as I join her and we go over to the door together.

"You know Gershom put him up to this," Calista says to Rosalind.

"You have proof of that?" Rosalind asks, her voice low.

"No, he's smarter than that," Calista says.

"Exactly," Rosalind says.

Calista's frown deepens. The waters here are deep. What is it about human nature that can create such hatred? Those of us who crashed in the other part of the ship didn't have politics like this going on. Survival was paramount. There wasn't time for such nonsense.

"Damn," Delilah says, keeping her voice low as she leans in close to the destroyed panel.

I'm not sure if she's talking about the damage or the overheard conversation from behind us. She looks over then darts her eyes back. Ah, the conversation, of course.

Biting my lower lip, I nod. I'm not sure what to make of it. Are the other humans here afraid of the Zmaj taking all their women? Is that what it is? If so, why do other women join that movement? It doesn't make sense. The Zmaj have been nothing but helpful. Even if Ladon was kind of scary outside the gate, he didn't act that way towards the humans.

"Yeah," I say, agreeing with Delilah.

"What the hell is wrong with these people?" she whispers.

"I don't know."

Delilah whistles a long, low sound as she digs through the wires.

"This is bad," she says. "When he smashed the lock it fried this circuit board. No way to repair that, we'll have to replace it."

"Great, wonder if they have one lying around somewhere?"

"Wouldn't that be nice?" Delilah says.

Snorting, I dig through the wires myself, looking for what, I don't know. The faint scent of burnt plastic is all the reward I get. She's right about the board being fried. I'm not an electronics expert but I've spent more than my fair share of time working on computers and I always stuck my nose in when the tech guys would do repairs.

"What's the verdict?" Rosalind asks.

"It's bad," Delilah says. "We need to replace that board there." She points behind the wires.

Rosalind nods but gives no sign of frustration. "Okay," she says.

"Damn it," Calista says, looking up and out the dome. "Ladon is out there."

I try to not let my thoughts go to Ragnar but it's like trying to deny gravity. There has to be an answer.

"Can we scavenge a board from something else?" I ask.

Calista shrugs.

"Well there were all those screens and electronics in that room you took me too," I say. "Are there more of those?"

Calista looks at Rosalind who nods.

"Good idea," Rosalind says. "Do it. Calista can you help them? Who's watching the baby?"

"He's with Jolie," Calista answers. "So yeah, I can help. I know nothing about electronics though."

"Right, lead them around the city. Take them to places we haven't commandeered yet."

"Is this the only gateway?" Delilah asks.

"No, but the other ones are on the opposite side of the city and what little power we have doesn't reach that far."

"Oh," Delilah says, shaking her head.

Turning to look out the dome I do a double take. Ragnar is standing right across from me. His hand presses against the iridescent dome.

My hand trembles as I reach out and press it against his. The dome is cold, lacking the warmth of his touch. An inch, maybe a touch more, is all that separates us. It might as well be miles.

I have to get this door open.

"Someone likes you," Delilah says, cutting through my moment.

My cheeks burn hot as I glance over my shoulder.

"Yeah," I say. "I guess so."

She smiles but doesn't say a thing more. It's moment like this that reinforces why she's my best friend.

"Let's get this door fixed," she says.

20

RAGNAR

Watching Olivia walk away from the dome cuts me. An open, bleeding wound, screaming my failure. She's on the other side. I didn't protect her.

My bijass rises so fast I don't feel its approach.

Pounding in my ears, my limbs tingle as blood rushes to them, my vision turns red.

Roaring, I slam my fists into the dome.

Tear it down. Must reach her.

She is mine!

A tiny human, inches away, grins. I'm going to tear that smile from his face.

He's one of them. One of those who took her from me.

Pounding the barrier, my fists are numb, it doesn't yield.

"Ragnar!" Bashir yells.

Ignore him.

Tear it down. Must reach Olivia.

My treasure. Mine.

I slam my tail and fists against the barrier over and over. Beyond pain. Numbness.

Nothing will stop me or stand in my way.

Hands grab my shoulders.

Jerking free I whirl, a new threat.

Bashir. His hands are raised, open, his tail low.

"Ragnar," he says.

"NO!" I scream.

"Together we are stronger," he says.

"She is mine," I hiss. "Mine!"

"Yes," Bashir says as Melchior approaches from my other side.

I move back, keeping them both in sight. They will not keep me from her.

"Edicts," Melchior says. "Ragnar, control yourself."

Their words cut through the red rage, finding me in the maelstrom of emotion. I watch as my body turns and I pound on the barrier again.

"OLIVIA!" I scream, but I'm a passenger to my anger, the bijass is in control.

"Edicts are edicts," Bashir says.

They keep their distance, talking, and their words penetrate the storm that roars around me. I am more than this.

I am myself.

"Edicts," Melchior repeats.

Turning to face them, the urge to make them submit rises. No one can stand against me. No one will keep Olivia from me.

"Edicts," Bashir says. "Together we are stronger."

Spreading my wings I throw my arms wide and scream my frustration at the stars above. Rage, anger, hurt, and loss pour out of me in one long display of emotion.

I let it all go until I am myself again. I am in control.

The rage fades, leaving an empty aching in my gut. "I must get to her."

"Of course," Bashir says.

"We'll help," Melchior adds.

The bond between us gives me strength. I draw on it, needing it.

"The Council will meet with Lana to discuss the events," Bashir says.

"Then let's invite ourselves," I say.

Bashir leads the way among the tents. The Tribe set them up in a circular pattern, the center of which is clear for gathering. Kalessin and Falkosh, the two Elders, and Visidion, the Commander, stand together. Visidion leans on his staff, staring at the ground. Drosdan stands to one side with his massive arms crossed over his chest. Lana, Astarot, and Ladon stand together.

My attention goes to Ladon first. He considers it his city, being locked out of it can't be sitting well with him.

The rest of the Tribe watches in a loose circle, keeping their distance. Normally the Council would meet in their cave if we were still in the valley and the Tribe could not listen. It's obvious they all want to know what is happening but are holding back from inserting themselves in the debate.

I have no such qualms. My female is on the wrong side of that dome. I will have answers.

Melchior and Bashir flank me as I cut through the crowd. I lead us to a stop, standing to one side of the Council and Lana and Astarot so we can see both groups.

"There is no doubt in my mind that Gershom put one of his followers up to this," Lana says.

"Who is this Gershom?" Falkosh, the Tribe Elder, asks.

"He's an asshole," Lana snaps.

The elders exchange a look at her brash, fast answer. Lana's sharp and doesn't miss it.

"Let me elaborate," she says, holding her hands up. "There are some of the humans who spout anti-Zmaj bullshit. They don't think we should work together. Especially if it means Zmaj men with Human women."

She looks at Astarot for affirmation who frowns and nods.

"Why is this a problem for them?" Visidion asks.

"Fear," Astarot interjects before Lana can speak. "They're scared, facing the doom of their race and have not had time to come to terms with it as we have. They fear that their females falling for our males will mean their end."

"That's entirely too nice a way to say it," Lana says, jumping back in. "That may be true for a lot of the followers but their leader, Gershom, really is an asshole. He doesn't buy the crap he spouts. He knows we need the Zmaj. Gershom is smart, don't underestimate his cunning. He wants power, and this is a way for him to get it."

"He puts his own gain and power above that of his people?" Visidion asks.

"He does," Lana says, without hesitation.

The Council Members look at each other but I watch Lana. Does she understand what she is doing?

"This Gershom, he manipulates the others of his tribe for power?" Visidion asks.

"That's exactly what he's doing," Lana says, crossing her arms over her chest.

A soft murmur passes around the circle.

"We believe that is what he is doing," Astarot says, softening her statement. "It is not something we can prove."

"How much proof do we need that the guy's a dickhole?" Lana snaps, throwing her arms up in the air. "He's been pulling shit since we landed here. Anything he can do to steal power from Rosalind."

"Rosalind is the leader of the humans?" Visidion asks.

"Yes," Lana says.

Anger pulses in my veins. If this Gershom is responsible for taking Olivia from me, he needs to learn the error of his ways.

"There is much to discuss," Visidion says.

"There is nothing to discuss," I interject.

Everyone turns to look at me.

"Hunter, you speak out of turn," the Commander says.

Stepping forward, I make a slashing motion with my hand through the air. "This Gershom has made his position clear," I say. "And he has cut me off from my treasure, the female that is mine."

I claim Olivia out loud for the first time.

"I hear your claim but-" Visidion starts to speak but is cut off as Kalessin steps forward to stand in the center.

"DANGER!" the Elder seer says, his voice roaring out with a power that drives deep in my bones.

All eyes go to him. Kalessin foresaw the devastation. His vision founded the Tribe, brought us together. He gave us the Edicts. No one dares interrupt him.

Astarot pulls Lana backwards, moving himself in front of her while looking around for any threat.

"Gershom will be the downfall of the Tribe," Kalessin says, his voice softer but somehow more sinister.

He shakes, shudders, then stands still.

No one dares a breath, waiting.

Kalessin straightens, then his form goes back to its normal stoop, and he slowly walks back to his position next to Falkosh.

Visidion steps forward two steps then taps his staff on the ground three times.

"That decides it. They must give us Gershom for trial and justice," he says.

"None of this gets us into the City," I say, stepping forward, the bijass pulsing through my veins.

I hold it at bay, reciting the Edicts in my head.

"I'm sure they're working on fixing the door," Lana says.

"Is there no other entrance?" I ask.

"The power grid isn't working well, or wasn't when we left. None of the other doors are powered."

"Can we dig under it?" I ask.

Lana looks at Astarot. He shrugs.

"I don't know," he says, looking at me.

"Then we will try," I say.

"That settles it," Visidion says. "Ragnar will be in charge of the digging. We will retrieve the females who wish to remain with us. The Tribe will not join the City until Gershom has seen justice."

Lana grins from ear to ear as if pleased with herself.

I don't think she understands what she has created. Gershom violates the Edicts if all she said is true. The Tribe will not tolerate it, we can't. The Edicts are our strength. Anyone who undermines them…

Shaking my head, I push the concern away. I have a dig to organize.

I'm coming Olivia.

21

OLIVIA

"Who about this?" I ask, pointing to a board deep inside one machine that Delilah and I are taking apart.

"Close, but no," she says, after inspecting it. "It doesn't have the same capacitor over here."

She moves her finger around one edge of the board.

"Oh, yeah, I see that," I agree.

Focusing on what's next keeps me going. Every time I stop, my thoughts turn to Ragnar. Is he okay? I know he's worrying and probably angry that he can't reach me. I'm worried about him too.

I can't believe that jerk did this. What did he hope to gain?

"You know what's dumb about this?" Delilah asks.

"Huh?"

"They need to get out of the dome too," she says. "I over-heard some of the girls before. They go out to hunt and gather that plant, the epis."

"Oh," I say, digging into yet another machine hoping it will have the part we need. I realize I've only been half paying attention to her. If I don't keep myself focused completely on the task, I can't do it because all I can think of is Ragnar.

Delilah stares at me with an arched eye before we dig back into our work.

"Here!" Delilah exclaims, holding a board up.

"Is that it?"

"I think so," she says, waving it around and grinning.

We get lost walking back to the gate but a friendly group points us in the right direction and it doesn't take long before we're back at the airlock.

There's two groups waiting when we arrive. On one side is Rosalind, Calista and two other women I don't know. Standing across from them is a group of five, three men, a woman, and Gershom himself. Neither group speaks as we walk up but both look at us. Nervous butterflies dance in my stomach. It feels like we're crossing an invisible barrier.

Delilah and I exchange furtive glances. Part of me wants to scream for them to quit looking at me or wave my arms wildly in the air or something. Anything to break the tension.

Something moves beyond the dome and I look out there for the first time. A group of five Zmaj walks towards the door, Ragnar among them. Drosdan stands out on size alone. Ladon is with them, too and the two other hunters.

They come to a stop a few feet away from the other side of the door. All five of the Zmaj cross their arms over their chests and stand staring, waiting.

"That looks ominous," Delilah mutters.

"Yeah," I agree. "Let's get this done."

We set to work. It takes time but Delilah knows her stuff. I contribute by holding wires but the first time she hooks it up it doesn't work. Something feels off. I take my time staring at it until the outpoint in the pattern stands out.

"Of course!" Delilah exclaims, when I point it out to her.

She adjusts the wires to fix the pattern. A soft whir comes from the panel then it lights up, ready for use.

"Yes!" I exclaim.

Delilah puts the broken panel back in place but we don't have any way to fasten it. She fiddles with it for a few minutes before giving up and letting them hang.

"Is it working?" Rosalind asks.

"Yeah," Delilah says.

Rosalind punches in a code and the inside door cycles open then shut. The rush of air fills the airlock then the far side opens. Anticipation makes me dance from foot to foot as I wait for Ragnar to walk into the airlock. I want his arms around me, his lips on mine, and I don't care who sees us.

As the air fills the chamber dividing inside the dome from outside, Ladon steps forward to stand in front of it. The other Zmaj, including Ragnar, continue to stand back. Swallowing hard, I try to stare my questions into Ragnar.

Why aren't you coming in? What is going on?

A tiny niggle of doubt forms in the back of my mind, worming its way through.

Doesn't he want me?

No, that can't be it.

But... I'm not as pretty, not as fit.

All the old doubts are there, waiting outside my walls of certainty I'd built with him. Ready to take me back into the mire.

The outside door closes and Ladon touches the panel inside the airlock, opening the inside door.

"This looks bad," Delilah whispers.

"Yeah."

Swallowing hard, I tear my eyes from Ragnar, doing my best to not cry. I don't know what's happening but it can't be as bad as the doubts in my head are making it. It can't be.

Ladon steps out then walks over to Rosalind.

"Ladon," Rosalind says, speaking Zmaj.

"Rosalind."

"Have you worked out your differences with the Tribe?" she asks.

"They have a demand," Ladon says.

"And what say you to their demand?" Rosalind asks, her eyes narrowing.

Something is so far off it's not even funny.

"The Tribe has a set of rules they call the Edicts. They will not take up residence with any who are unwilling to follow their Edicts," Ladon says.

"And what are these Edicts?" Rosalind asks.

"One, I am myself. Two, together we are stronger. Three, survival of the group matters."

"Fine," Rosalind says, then shakes her head. "What does this have to do with us?"

"Lana has made it clear to them that there are those in the City who do not accept the Zmaj. This is clear by the actions of the one who broke the door."

"Common, can we get a translation Rosalind?" Gershom interjects.

"Wait," she barks. "What is it they want?" she asks Ladon.

"They want Gershom," he says.

"Or?" Rosalind asks.

"Or what?" Ladon responds.

"Right. Or what?" she asks again.

"If we do not give them Gershom, for trial and justice, they will not move into the City."

"I see," Rosalind says.

That's why the others are staying outside. Looking over my shoulder, Ragnar is waiting there, refusing to come in. Proud, strong, and loyal.

"Rosalind, this is ridiculous. I demand to know what is

being said," Gershom says, the small group with him muttering their support.

"We should discuss this in private," Rosalind says to Ladon. "The Council will meet," she says in Common, "in thirty minutes. I'll relay the message then."

"I wonder what that's all about," Delilah says.

"The Tribe wants Gershom," I whisper.

"You're kidding, wait, how do you know?"

"I can speak Zmaj now."

"No shit?" she exclaims.

"Yeah, no shit," I say, worry making my stomach a tight knot.

"Are you coming?" Calista asks.

"Huh?" I ask, jumping as she speaks.

"You coming?" she repeats. "You should both attend the Council meeting."

"Us? We're not part of this," I answer.

"Sure you are," Calista says. "You've got as much stake in this as anyone. Your man is on the outside, your voice matters too."

Locking eyes with Delilah we both nod to Calista.

"Okay, where do we go?"

ROSALIND SITS AT THE HEAD OF A LARGE TABLE. DELILAH AND I sit on the right, which appears to be the side of those that don't dig Gershom. Gershom and his supporters sit opposite.

"So that is what they want," Rosalind says, having just relayed the Tribe's demands.

"Ridiculous," Gershom says. "I had nothing to do with this."

"The situation is clear," Rosalind says, speaking in both

Common and Zmaj to make sure everyone understands. "They want what they demand."

"Why would we give them anything? They need us, we don't need them!" Gershom says.

"Don't we?" Rosalind asks, after translating his words for the Zmaj.

"They have hunters, our food supplies are dangerously low. They have craftsmen. We don't know how many of the survivors from the other part of the ship might stay with them too," Rosalind observes.

What do I do? I have to wonder myself. Staying in the city would be nice but could I do it without Ragnar? Will I have a choice?

"Bah, let them," Gershom says. "If we give in to their demands now what does that say about us? I thought Ladon claimed this city is his and no other's. Is he going to let these other Zmaj tell him what to do?"

Rosalind looks to Ladon and translates.

"If they are right, they are right," Ladon says. "But in this case, we have no way to prove that Gershom did anything. If they asked for the perpetrator, that I could live with. Giving them Gershom I cannot do. Not without proof he ordered this."

Rosalind stares, her frown growing deeper. "I wish you were wrong," she says in Zmaj. "If I hand Gershom over, half the City would riot. He has too many supporters and if we can't present clear cut evidence to them, we'd be in trouble."

"Let's not forget about translating!" Gershom interjects, his voice loud and annoying.

Rosalind closes her eyes and her lips move slightly like she's counting to herself before she turns to face Gershom.

"Ladon says we can't hand you over without proof," Rosalind says.

"Well, that's a surprising level of sensibility," Gershom says. "Thank you."

"Sverre, what do you think?" Rosalind asks the other Zmaj.

"I have Jolie and our baby to think of," Sverre says. "While I think the City would be better off without Gershom in the long run, I can't risk the trouble it would bring to have him handed over without obvious cause."

"Olivia?" Rosalind asks, singling me out.

My eyes go wide and my throat dries up when she calls on me. Shaking my head and looking around, I don't know how to respond.

"Yes?" I ask, swallowing hard and trying to force moisture back into my mouth.

"What is your opinion? How much trouble will this cause between us and the Tribe?"

My mind is racing. I don't know how to answer. "I don't know," I say as honestly as I can.

"And those of you that traveled here with them, what will you do?" Rosalind asks.

Ragnar isn't going to come in without the Tribe and I'm not going to stay without him. Glancing over my shoulder at Delilah, she squeezes my hand under the table and nods.

"We will go with the Tribe if they don't come in the City," I answer at last.

"Damn," Rosalind says.

"Bah, we don't need them," Gershom says. "We're getting along fine now."

"Don't we?" Rosalind asks, her eyes narrowing. "They have an engineer, a real one. And a doctor, a human doctor. You don't think that might be useful?"

Gershom opens his mouth then snaps it shut.

"Ladon, what will they do when we say no?" Rosalind asks.

Ladon purses his lips, his hand resting on the table flexing open and closed. "I'm not sure," he says. "They can't get into the city, so we're safe there, but I don't think they would resort to violence anyway."

"That's good, at least," she says. "Fine, all in favor of we tell them no?"

They vote by show of hands. Delilah and I don't cast a vote but the motion carries. They will not turn over Gershom.

"I'll tell them," Rosalind says, rising. "Olivia, Delilah will you walk with me?"

The nervous butterflies explode in my stomach again. Nodding, I stumble as I rise from the table then we both fall in with the Lady General. She leads us out of the Council chamber in silence. Only when we're outside and alone does she speak.

"I don't suppose I could talk either of you into staying?" she asks.

I exchange a long look with Delilah. "I'm honored," I say, "but there's a member of the Tribe I don't want to live without."

Rosalind nods, looking over to Delilah.

"She's my best friend," Delilah says, like that says it all.

22

RAGNAR

*T*he humans approach the gate. My hearts speed up seeing Olivia walking next to the female in white. Delilah walks next to them as the three talk in what appears to be a friendly manner. Ladon is a step behind them, looking grim.

"Shit," Lana says.

She and Astarot are standing behind me. Bashir and Melchior flank me, standing right behind Visidion and Drosdan.

"What?" I ask her.

"He's not with them," she says.

Looking again, she's right. Gershom is not with the group approaching the gate. All of the females that arrived with us are but there is no sign of Gershom.

The gate cycles open but time moves at a crawl. Anticipation is making my scales itch. They can't be doing what I think they are. Thoughts race through my mind as I work to figure out our next move. What will Visidion do?

We can't live in a city that allows violation of the Edicts. It would undermine everything that makes the Tribe work. We'd regress, lose ourselves to the bijass.

The woman in white leads, coming out of the airlock. She marches up with the others forming a line behind her. I lock eyes with Olivia. She's biting her lower lip, her hands twitch, she's nervous.

The bijass stretches its fingers into my mind, seeking cracks in my defenses. Reciting the Edicts, I keep it at bay but if they try to take her from me...

"Commander Visidion," the female in white says, stopping ten feet in front of him. "I am Rosalind, leader of the humans of Drakonov."

"Welcome Rosalind," Visidion says, stepping close into her personal space. While not the largest of the Zmaj, his size is imposing compared to the human female. "I hope you bring good news that will bring our peoples together."

Rosalind doesn't flinch or move away, she matches his dominance with her own. Interesting.

"We have considered your request. We cannot, in good conscience, honor it," she says.

"I see," Visidion says, lowering his face close to hers. "This is your final answer?"

"Our Council has voted, this is not up for discussion," Rosalind says, but do I detect something else in her voice?

Olivia is all but vibrating, I can feel the barely contained emotions raging inside her despite the distance between us. What does this mean for us? Will they try to keep her?

Visidion breathes deeply and his chest nearly touches the white-clad human female. Does she shudder?

"Okay," Visidion says. He turns so that his mouth is close to Rosalind's ear. "We will not take up residence in your city. I request you allow our people to return to us and we will be on our way." His voice is low and soft.

"Surely we can work this out," Rosalind says, turning so that her face is mere inches from the Commander's.

Ladon crosses his arms and turns his head to the side. An outward sign he's unwilling to negotiate further.

"No," Visidion murmurs while staring at the female. "Our people cannot live without the Edicts. I will not expose them to violations or put my people at risk. It is obvious our differences are great, too great to work out easily."

"I see," Rosalind says. "What does this mean for our future?"

"The future is ever changing," Visidion answers. "We will leave peacefully, as long as you return our people to us."

"I can't do that," Rosalind says.

The murmurs of conversation stops.

Drosdan hisses, a low and dangerous sound as he steps forward, his massive hands balling into fists. Ladon, his wings spreading out part way, steps forward to meet him.

"Wait!" Rosalind says, holding a hand up but not putting any space between herself and the Commander.

"What is this?" Visidion nearly hisses in her ear. "You would take what is ours and deny us entry?"

"No," Rosalind replies. "That is not my intent. I would ask that the human females who came with you have a choice. Any Zmaj of the Tribe may make the same choice. They can stay with us, live in the city, as long as they will contribute they would be welcome."

Drosdan hisses again and takes another step forward. Ladon matches his movement.

"Stop," Visidion says, his voice is quiet, but it carries well. He still has not taken his eyes from Rosalind.

Drosdan stops, looking over his shoulder to the Commander. Visidion motions with his staff and Drosdan returns to his place, shoulders slumped, but he doesn't even think about disobeying.

My lungs won't take air, waiting in anticipation for what comes next. I'm ready to lead the attack if I have to. With small hand gestures, I make my intent clear and Bashir and Melchior are ready too. I'll take Olivia by force if I have to. She is mine.

"Free choice?" Visidion growls.

"Yes," Rosalind replies.

Vibrations run through my muscles as my body prepares, ready to move into action. I visualize possibilities, dozens and dozens of them, preparing for every outcome. No matter what happens, I'm ready.

"Okay," Visidion says. "Give the females their choice."

"And the Zmaj?" Rosalind asks, pressing the issue.

"None of the Tribe will live outside the Edicts," Visidion says, no hint of a doubt in his voice.

He's right. We won't. The Edicts are our life, they bring us together, keep us from falling to the bijass. That any of us would choose otherwise is outside the realm of the possible.

Rosalind's jaw tightens. Finally she puts a small space between herself and Visidion, turning her back to him and facing the females behind her. Before she can say a word, Olivia runs.

Ladon's eyes widen, Drosdan turns to face a possible threat, taking a step forward.

"Ragnar!" she yells.

My hearts explode into double time, pounding in my chest, blood rushing to my limbs and head. I'm running towards her then she's in my arms. Sweeping her off her feet I encircle her in my wings as our lips smash together with bruising force. I want to drink her in, claim her here and now. She is mine, my treasure, never again will I let her anyone part us.

Our kisses are hungry, edged with desperation and need. Her presence fills an empty ache. She is my everything. Her arms are around my neck, her lips on mine, my hands on her rear.

She pulls back. "I love you," she says.

"I love you," I say, then everything stops.

My eyes widen, my mouth drops open, and my hearts don't beat.

She spoke to me.

Zmaj.

Perfect Zmaj.

She laughs, kissing me, with quick soft pecks of her lips.

"I love you Ragnar, my perfect, beautiful male," she says.

"How..."

She laughs, the sound of her voice music to my ears.

"A machine," she says. "We can talk. At last!"

"You are my treasure," I say, my hearts soaring. "You are perfect."

My chest expands and I know at any moment I will explode. A body isn't made to contain such emotions.

"Always," she says, between our kisses.

Her fingers trail over my cheeks, down my neck and arms. Moisture streams down her face from her perfect, beautiful eyes, and still we kiss.

Finally filling the void of missing her, I set her on her feet. We kiss one last time before I fold my wings and let the outside world back in.

All of the other human females who traveled with us have crossed over from Rosalind's side to stand behind Visidion.

"This is not the end," Rosalind says, holding her arm out to Visidion.

"Every day brings choices," Visidion agrees as he takes her arm.

"We need each other," Rosalind says. "Is there no way we can resolve these differences?"

"Yes," Visidion purrs. "Give us this Gershom."

"I can't," Rosalind says, her regret obvious.

"We will find a home," Visidion says. "I'll send a messenger once we have."

"Okay," Rosalind says.

Something passes between the two leaders. Their grip on each other's arms seems to linger, their eyes stare into each other. Visidion leans in and says something no one else can hear.

Neither moves for an extended moment.

Eventually, Visidion turns and walks away and the Tribe sets to work, packing up tents. The females coming with us stand in a huddle. Olivia grips my hand tight before she walks away to join them.

Astarot and Lana are talking with Rosalind. Almost, I think they're arguing, then Rosalind's shoulders drop. Lana embraces several of the females from the City. Astarot and Ladon embrace then part. Lana joins the other females remaining with the Tribe and Astarot comes over towards me.

"Ragnar," he says.

"Astarot," I answer.

"Perhaps you could use another hunter?" he asks.

Glancing at Bashir and Melchior, they both nod their agreement before I put an arm out. Astarot grips my arm and we shake before I pull him into an embrace.

"Welcome," I say.

"Thanks," he answers.

"We need to get busy, the Tribe needs a home."

"Lana and I have an idea," Astarot says, smiling.

THE JOURNEY SOUTH IS SLOW. MOVING SO MANY PEOPLE, especially with the females, isn't easy. By the time the suns are setting I can see mountains on the horizon. We stop for the night and make camp.

"Take the tent," Bashir says, a grin on his face. "Melchior and I will sleep out here."

Melchior pats me on the back then they go a distance away and set themselves up to sleep.

"What was that?" Olivia asks, having finished putting away our cookware.

"We have the tent to ourselves," I say, unable to keep the grin off my face.

"Oh," she says, grinning too.

We don't waste time climbing into the shelter. As the flap falls behind us her hands are on me, diving into my pants and grabbing my cock. She strokes me while I strip the layers of her clothes off. We kiss, passionate, deep kisses as our hands explore each other finding the points that bring each other pleasure.

Lying her down on the blankets I kiss my way down her beautiful, perfect body. She tenses as I kiss along her sides, suppressing laughter.

"That tickles," she says.

I adjust my kisses, moving to a less sensitive path as I make my way towards my goal.

The soft scent of her fills my nostrils, building my arousal higher. Desire pounds in my blood pushing me to hurry. Mastering it, I let it build while working my way around her core. Licking along her delicate lips then down her legs and back up towards her center.

She wriggles under my ministrations. As I continue kissing up and across her I tease her lips open with a finger, dipping it into her wetness.

"Ragnar," she groans.

My cock pulses in response, desire flaring as she says my name.

Unable to control myself any longer I drive my finger deep into her while lapping her folds with my tongue. Curling my finger inside her and finding the hard nub with my tongue. Her nails dig into my shoulders as her back arches, driving her up.

Flattening my tongue against her I lick up and down while wiggling my finger. She tenses, hips buck, then she's thrusting up into me with a wild abandon. I push her until she's over the edge. Her muscles quiver as her pleasure rips through her body.

Hooking my free arm around her waist I hold her close until it passes, and she relaxes.

"Take me," she says.

Sliding up, my cock goes straight into her. Her eyes widen, her mouth forms an O, and she cries out in pleasure. My eyes close as her body grips my cock tight, taking me in one smooth slide, burying myself in her.

Her fingers lace behind my neck. Our bodies rise and fall together, coming into each other and out as we join. Panting pleasure, we find our rhythm, joining until desire overtakes me. She thrusts up as I drive in and then I'm exploding my love into her, filling her with it.

Our foreheads rest against each other. Together we are stronger.

She is my more, more than I knew I needed.

She is my life.

OLIVIA

*R*ed, jagged stone pushes up out of the ground, breaking across the skyline. The mountain looks like broken teeth sticking up to form a shape like birds in flight.

We have to march clear around and come up into the bowl shape from the bottom side, adding about half a day to our travel time. Lana and Astarot knew the way to get us here because this is the source of epis for the City.

How will they react to us moving into their epis caves? It's like taking away control of the thing they all still need to survive here.

There's a large opening that drives down in the middle of the massive rocky mountain right ahead, it doesn't look inviting or friendly. It's dark, like a giant maw ready to swallow us.

Ragnar insisted that he and the hunters go through first to make sure it's safe. Having fallen into a nest of guster gives me all the reason I need to agree with him.

It doesn't take very long for them to return, dirty but safe, and the caves are ready for us to claim.

"Well, here we go," Delilah says.

"Yeah, great, why did we leave the city again?" Astrid asks.

"I'm here for my daughter, Lana," Bailey says, smiling. "I love her but yeah, this decision of hers…" Her smile makes it clear she's joking.

"I'm here for you," Penelope says to Astrid. "I didn't want to stay back there all alone."

"Yeah, me too," Delilah says. "I'm here for my bestie."

She nods over at me, but her side-long glances at a certain Zmaj say that even though what she's saying may be part of the truth, it's a long way from all of it.

"Okay girls," I say. "Let's get started, we have a lot to do if we're going to make this our new home."

"Look at how that path leads up the rocks there," Delilah says, pointing. "There are small cracks up there that might open into caves we could use for individual homes."

"Yeah," I say. "We should get with Errol. He's the mason that built most of the Valley for the Tribe. I bet he could show us how to work with the natural formations here to make homes."

We walk into the main cave while talking. It's a massive open space and our voices echo around.

"Well that's annoying," I observe.

"Yeah, HELLO!" Delilah yells, grinning over her shoulder.

HELLO - HELLO - hello - hello - hell comes the echo.

Rolling my eyes, I shake my head as she laughs.

"If we collect furs, we could use them to dampen the sound," Astrid says. "Hang them on the walls somehow."

"Oh, good idea," Penelope says. "That would be nice for our individual spaces too, we could use it like carpet."

"Yes," I agree. "I like that idea a lot."

"So this can be the common area?" Penelope asks. "Like the outdoors in the valley."

"I think that's perfect," I say, and for the first time I notice that the girls keep looking at me any time they present an idea.

When did that happen?

Lana is more a leader than I am. I'm just me.

Padraig walks into the cave then up to our small group. The Tribe smith is big, burly, and always comes off a bit gruff but I suspect behind the snarly exterior is a big teddy bear.

"Are you females going to use the small cave to the south of the entrance? I want that for my forge," he crosses his arms across his massive chest.

"Okay? No?" I say, making it a question because he's looking right at me.

"Good," he says then turns and walks away.

Looking at the other girls I arch an eyebrow and they all laugh.

"What?" I ask. "He just asked my permission to use a cave and I have no idea why."

"The look on your face," Delilah says, gasping around her laughter.

"Yeah?"

"Oh, Olivia," Astrid says. "You're so sweet."

Embarrassment flushes my cheeks. I shake my head side to side, unsure of what's going on or why I'm the center of attention.

"I don't get it," I say.

"That's for sure," Penelope says, laughing harder.

"Bailey?" I ask, hoping the older woman might shed some light.

"Olivia, honey," she says, putting an arm on mine. "You're our de facto leader. We look to you now. Isn't it obvious?"

"Uh, no? Why?" It feels like the weight of the world just landed on my shoulders. I'm not ready for this. "What about Lana? She's the leader here, not me."

"My daughter is a hunter, that is what she wants," Bailey

173

says. "She'll be out with Astarot and the other men. You're the only one of us that will be here who speaks Zmaj. There wasn't time for the rest of us to learn it in all that happened. By default that makes you our leader."

"But I'm no-"

"Yes, you are," Delilah says, cutting her own laughter off. "You never see it do you? All of us have talked about it. You're perfect and you're the one we want."

Ahhh! Ok girl, get yourself together, you can do this.

"Okay," I smile.

"So, back to what we were working on," Penelope says. "If we make this a common area, we could set up sections for doing work we all need."

"What work are you thinking of?" I ask.

"Anything that would be better to do in company," she says. "Preparing food for storage, making clothes, crafting work."

We walk the length of the cave as we walk. At the back there's a crack in the wall through which shines a faint blue glow. The slit is tall but narrow, just wide enough that the smaller girls could slip through it, I will have to turn sideways and work my boobs to fit. Everyone stops shy of entering.

"We'll make our homes in the smaller caverns up and down the cliff face then?" Astrid asks.

"That's what I was thinking," Penelope says. "What do you think Olivia?"

"It sounds fine," I say.

"Those of us who don't have a… mate?" Astrid turns her statement into a question and looks at me.

My cheeks burn hot and I can't meet any of their eyes. "Yep," I say, pushing the attention away. "That's what the Zmaj call it."

Mates sounds so… primal. It makes me feel, owned, in a

good way though. I'm his, claimed by Ragnar. He's everything I have ever dreamed of and more. Seriously, what girl ever dreamed of a dragon-man, one with two... well yeah. I know I didn't, not in my wildest fantasies.

Blood rushes to my face and my ears burn. Damn, I embarrass myself without saying a word.

"So yeah, those of us who aren't mated can share a space, just like on the ship," Astrid says, picking up where she left off.

"Oh, I like that," Delilah says. "I don't think I could sleep alone. It'd be too strange, you know?"

"It's a good solution," Bailey says.

"Well I'm not going to live in a bare stone cave," Penelope says. "Can we work out some comforts?"

"We've got blankets," Delilah says. "But that's not living in comfort."

"The thicker furs off those... what do they call those things? The ones that look like overgrown buffalo with teeth and a weird mutation?" Bailey asks.

"Bivo?" I ask, guessing at what she means.

"I think so, yeah. Those have the thick fur. If the hunters could gather that for us, we could start out making bedding. If we treat it and preserve the fur, then we could use those in place of a mattress."

"That's good," Astrid agrees.

"Where's Arawn, he's the leather worker, he'll know if we could do that," I say.

"Which one is Arawn?" Penelope asks.

I describe him to her and she smiles with a spark in her eye. "Oh, yeah, I saw him outside working on something."

"Okay, I'll talk to him later then," I say.

"Storage, that will be the next thing," Astrid says.

"Could we weave something? Make baskets?" Penelope asks.

"What would we weave?" Bailey asks. "Problem with this whole damn planet is there's not that much material to work with."

"Astarot says there's an oasis not far from here to the west," I say. "The one that Ragnar and I stopped at after we got lost in the storm had a lot of plants. Surely this one would have something we could use as material for weaving."

"A trip to the oasis then?" Delilah asks.

"We'll have to coordinate that with Ragnar, too dangerous to go on our own."

Everyone gives their agreement.

"So, since we're standing outside the entrance here," Bailey says, nodding at the crevasse in the wall.

All of us fall silent, looking at the tight opening. The faint blue glow emanating through it is a siren's call. It's been on everyone's mind, though we've avoided talking about it.

Epis.

We are living in the closest supply, giving us easy access. It also puts us in charge of the easiest source, which the city needs. This wasn't necessarily our plan, but it puts us in a good position.

"This is our home," I say. "Nothing will change that. We should make the best of it."

A murmur of agreement goes around.

Happiness swells inside me.

"What are you grinning about?" Delilah asks.

"This, you, us," I say, shaking my head. "Look at us! We're going to be okay. More than that, this will be good."

"Yeah," Delilah says and we all resume walking around the cavern.

"I feel it too," Penelope says. "The ship wreck was good, but I never felt hope for the future. It was just survival, you know?"

"Oh, yeah, that's it!" Astrid agrees. "It's like there's something more than surviving. A reason to live. Hope."

As we walk out of the cavern, back into the bright double red suns of Tajss, a sense of well being washes over me. Looking out across the rolling sands, I'm home. I've found my place and for the first time in my life I'm happy.

RAGNAR

"The females are helping to build a smoking station in that cavern over there," I say pointing.

"Okay," Bashir says.

He and Melchior carry a stretcher between them that we've loaded with harvested meat and leather. It's been a good hunt. We have enough food here to feed the Tribe for a week or more. Olivia will be happy with the furs we've brought.

Shadows are falling as the suns set and the soft glow of a fire emanates from our new home.

The females will probably have a meal ready but I need to do something first. Olivia will understand.

Turning away, I climb the tight, crumbling path up the cliff opposite ours. It turns back and forth as I make my way until I'm near the top. The cavern I approach has a metal grate attached to the rock wall, courtesy of Padraig. It's made of scavenged metal from the wreck of the human ship. It's less than a day's walk for a Zmaj and our smith brought several pieces back and is excited to continue working with it. I've never seen him so happy. He's talking about trying to make actual lochabers. I haven't wielded a lochaber in years, my fingers itch to grasp the hilt of one once more.

Humming comes from beyond the metal gate. My brother's tune is familiar, but I can't quite place it.

The sound stops and the memories it calls fade back into oblivion.

A metal rod hooks the clasp of the gate which I work open and it screeches as I pull it aside.

The clank of chains resounds heavily in the now silence and stepping into the shadows of the cavern, I brace myself.

Will he attack me today?

Ryuth sits at the back, staring at nothing. He doesn't react to my presence.

"Hello brother," I offer.

Still nothing.

Sighing, I pull out chunks of my recent kill. When I hold them out on my palm his eyes move, the only sign that he knows I'm here. We have to keep him bound so he can't feed himself. Leaning in, moving slow, I raise the meat to his lips.

I've lost count of how many times he's bitten me. It's the way it is. I don't know what the Zzlo did to break him, but I will reach him. I know he's in there, somewhere.

"We had a good hunt," I say, searching his eyes for any hint of recognition.

His stare is blank, empty. He takes the piece of meat when I press it to his lips. I watch him chew while I talk about my hunt. He swallows the last of the meat and I rise, backing my way out. Even though he's chained, he's still dangerous. Fully in the grip of his bijass, I can never let my guard down around him.

As I slide the gate closed, he is watching me. When I turn away, he hums the same tune as when I approached.

Then it hits me, I remember where I heard it before!

Turning, I rush back to the gate, staring in. The moment I'm at the gate he stops humming, staring into space.

"Ryuth?" I ask, hoping beyond hope for him to answer.

Nothing. He remains stock still, eyes fixed on something in the space ahead.

My stomach sinks as I walk away but now I have a glimmer of hope. That tune is one our mother hummed to us when we were children.

Locked inside, somewhere, is my brother and I will find him.

THE MAIN CAVE IS A BUSTLE OF ACTIVITY. THE FEMALES AND A few craftsmen have constructed a smoke pit on the left side. Bashir and Melchior are there helping them load the freshly harvested meat onto the racks. Olivia glances over as I walk in then she runs to me.

"Hi!" she says, throwing her arms around my neck, our lips coming together with rising passion.

"Hi," I respond as soon as she comes up for air.

"I missed you," she says.

We walk back to the others with our arms around each other.

"We're going to need better storage," Olivia says.

One female says something and Olivia answers her. They banter back and forth while I pitch in, helping lay the meat out on the carefully built racks. Olivia stops, cocks her head to one side, then frowns.

"Ragnar," she says, grabbing my attention. "Have the Zmaj tried growing things?"

"Growing what things?" I ask.

"Food stuffs," she says.

"Why would we do that? It grows just fine in the oasis."

Olivia snorts and says something to the females in their language before returning to me.

"You're such a male," she says.

"What else would I be?" I ask, confused by her statement.

She shakes her head. "Never mind. So the answer is no, hmmm."

The females talk amongst themselves. Bashir, Melchior and I exchange glances wondering what they are planning. The other two hunters say nothing and I shrug in response.

"So we have an idea," Olivia says at last.

"Yes?" I ask.

"Well, there's water down where the epis grows, and sandy dirt. Maybe we can find edible plants that will grow down there."

"It's dark," I observe.

"Sure," she says. "But maybe we can work it out. Or maybe we can get it to grow outside the cave. I don't know, isn't it worth a shot?"

"Would it make you happy?" I ask.

"Yes," she smiles, her cheeks flushing a luscious shade of pink.

"Then I'll see it done," I say. "We'll go to the oasis in the morning."

The females converse while we finish loading the meat. When it's almost done Bashir, Melchior and I leave them to finish and go help Arawn with the leather we brought back. It needs scraping, which removes any remnants of flesh before it spoils. It's full dark by the time we're done. My limbs are heavy, I'm exhausted. Olivia and I head to the private cave we claimed.

I pull aside the leather hanging that gives us some sense of privacy, letting her in first. She ducks as she enters, her full ass brushing against my cock. She laughs, glancing over her shoulder with a smile.

"I thought you'd be too tired?"

"I'm never too tired for you," I say, pulling her close.

Her body molds against mine. Kissing my way down her neck and across her shoulder, I caress my way around her hips and across her stomach. She wraps her arms around my neck. Moving as one we make our way to the blankets and I lower her into them.

OLIVIA

"What about these?" I ask, pointing at a purple-blue berry looking thing.

"Those are edible but very sour," Ragnar says.

We work together and carefully dig it up, taking great care to make sure we get all the roots then add it to the stretcher with the other plants.

"This looks like enough," I say, wiping sweat from my brow.

"Good," Ragnar says. "We need to head back, I don't want to be out after dark."

Bashir and Ragnar take up the stretcher and we head for home, the shadows are growing long when at last we enter the main cave.

"Welcome home!" Delilah says.

"Thanks!"

Astrid and Penelope come over and look at the plants we've gathered.

"We prepared the ground outside for them," Astrid says. "And Padraig crafted two buckets for us to haul water out of the caves to water them with."

"Oh, nice," I say.

Lana walks by with Astarot. She waves as they pass by, working on their own projects. I haven't seen much of her because we've all been so busy. Something about her catches my attention. I can't quite put my finger on it...

"Let's get these in the ground," Penelope says.

Bashir and Ragnar follow Penelope outside with the stretcher and set it down next to the turned earth.

"We had to dig down quite a ways to find actual dirt and we hauled out quite a lot of soil from inside the cavern hoping it would help encourage things to grow," Astrid says, motioning her arm around the turned area.

It's a square about twelve feet long and four feet wide. It drops two feet down. Stiff leather with steel bars reinforces it every few feet.

"Wow, that's a lot of work girls," I say.

Ragnar grabs me by my waist and kisses me. "I'll be back," he says, glancing up the mountain.

It's time for him to feed Ryuth.

"See you at home love," I say.

He nods then heads up to feed his brother.

"Thanks," Astrid says. "I think it came out great."

"Good idea, reinforcing the walls with leather. I wondered how we'd get around the sand wanting to slide back in."

"Thank Arawn, that was his idea, oh and Padraig helped too of course," Penelope says.

"Yeah, Padraig did most of the digging," Astrid says.

"No wonder you got so much done so fast," I say.

"Isn't he dreamy?" Delilah asks, her voice betraying a hint of wistfulness that makes me smile.

"Has anyone heard anything from the City?" Penelope asks, while we work on getting the plants into the ground.

"Nothing," I say, then out of nowhere it hits me. "Holy shit!"

"What?" both girls ask.

"Lana, oh my god, Lana!"

"What? What about her?" Astrid asks.

"You two haven't noticed?"

Astrid and Penelope look at each other than shake their heads.

"No?" they say.

"She's pregnant," I say.

"No way!" Penelope exclaims.

"You're sure? How do you know?" Astrid asks.

"Look at her, she's showing," Delilah says, laughing.

"That's amazing," Penelope says.

A warm fire burns in my stomach. A baby. Wouldn't that be nice? I can't shake the idea or the ticking in the back of my head while we finish working. Once we're done I head for home, determined to make a shot at having one of my own.

Our cave is half-way up the cliff and I stop to look out over our home before going in.

Home.

Beautiful. Simple, but ours. Maybe living in the city would be nice but I don't think it could be any nicer than what we're building here. This is ours. All of us, working together and creating a new life. And soon there will be a new life too.

Goosebumps race across my skin thinking about it.

Turning I pull aside the leather flap that serves as our door. As soon as I do, Ragnar takes my arm and pulls me into an embrace.

"Hi," I say, kissing his sweet lips.

"I've missed you," he says.

"You just saw me," I laugh.

"That changes nothing," he says, between kisses.

His hands roam down my back and across my ass.

I shiver as heat blazes through my body. My nipples harden and my pussy tingles as it grows warm and wet.

"Mmm," a moan slips out as he presses his hard cock against my ass.

"Are you happy?" he asks.

"I am," I say, running my fingers through his hair.

"You are mine," his voice is soft, almost a growl.

My head spins, breath catches in my throat as he claims what is his, then he scoops me up into his arms.

Turning around he carries me effortlessly to the bed, his tongue pushing past my eager lips to find mine.

Eagerly he jerks my shirt up and over my head, the only break in his lips against mine to let it pass.

He buries his face between my breasts. I gasp, adrenaline and desire spiking through me as he ravages my body with his mouth.

Stepping back his eyes move over my naked body, drinking me in.

"You're so beautiful," he says, his voice low and husky.

His hands slide over my skin, pulling me close. I fall into his lips and let my hands explore his rock-hard chest, chiseled abs and the hard grooves of his hips. His scales are cool to the touch as I work my way lower.

He leans into me and I moan, feeling the huge thickness between his legs pressing hot and powerfully against my belly. My fingers move lower, feeling his huge cock, unable to grasp its girth fully in my hand.

He groans.

"Like this?" I whisper in his ear, kissing my way down his cheek while moving my hand up and down his massive shaft.

"Mmm," he groans, his hips thrust against me. "You unleash me. I can't control myself with you."

"Then don't," I say. "I trust you."

His eyes flash fire and his cock throbs in my hand.

I shriek as we suddenly tumble backwards onto the blankets. My heart pounds in my chest and desire spikes through me.

He looms over me, his muscles bunching and his jaw tight. His eyes lock with mine as he moves between my legs, his first cock pressing against my opening.

I'm more turned on then I've ever been before, his presence is dominating.

"Mine," he hisses, pushing his cock into my soft folds.

My eyes roll back in my head as he enters me up to the first ridge of his cock. Done going slow, he drives into my soaking wet pussy.

Nothing stops him, he takes me.

"Ragnar!" I cry his name as his humongous cock drives deep into my core.

"My treasure," he growls.

His lips take mine just as his cock takes my pussy. Wetness soaks out of me, drenching both of us as my pussy welcomes him . He holds himself over me, buried to his hilt.

He rotates his hips, a small circle, grinding the hard ridge at the base of his cock against my clit.

"OH GOD!" I scream in pleasure.

There is no control. I groan, then my orgasm claims me. My pussy clamps down on his massive cock. Every ridge of his huge dick swells inside. Liquid fire burns from my vagina through my limbs.

Stars and sensation wipe away thought. My pussy throbs with pleasure, clenching and unclenching, milking his cock and filling me with his seed.

Shuddering, reason returns slowly. He holds me tight, strong arms and bulging muscles carrying me through the power of my orgasm.

His cock softens inside me.

Smiling, a plan in my mind, I push against him. Slowly he slides out, rising back onto his knees.

He's kneeling between my legs as I sit back, a grin on my face.

His second cock rises, standing upright, pulsating its need for attention.

He just stretched my pussy and sated me but lust drives me still. Crawling towards him I work my way towards his beautiful cock, studying the vein that runs the length of the unprotected underside.

Slowly I open my mouth as I approach, wanting to taste him *so* badly.

Ragnar leans back, resting on his arms with his legs underneath, pushing his hips out so his cock is pointing at me, ready.

As the head of his massive cock touches my lips, somehow I fall under a spell, hypnotized by him. A shiver runs through my body, I'm trembling and my pussy is throbbing with a fresh growing need as I open my mouth and push my lips over his thick head.

I can't take much of him into my mouth, his size is too great. I wrap my lips around what I can and suck hard.

Ragnar groans, hissing in pleasure as his hand slides into my hair, making me smile and feel bold.

I suck harder at his head, letting my spit and his sweet, tangy juices drip copiously down his thick, pulsing shaft.

I stroke up and down with both my hands as though I'm greasing a pole.

My moans join his as I suck, the head of his cock soft and velvety against my lips. The underside is hot skin with small pulsing veins that let me feel the power in it, sending a jolt to my core.

Sliding down his shaft I find his balls, swollen and tight, and softly I play with them.

"Yes!" he exclaims as I do. "There, yes my treasure."

His hand tightens in my hair but he doesn't force me. His free hand reaches down, stroking my skin, his fingers roll over my rock hard nipples sending a jolt of pleasure through me.

Moving down I slide my lips along the unprotected underside of his shaft, my lips and tongue lapping at his veined shaft, bathing it in my spit.

Ragnar groans, then throws his head back and hisses. My pussy is a dull ache, ready to fill again, but I'm not done with him yet.

Raw primal desire rips through my body and it takes all my control to not throw myself on top and let him finish inside me.

He grips my shoulders, pulling my mouth off his cock. Our eyes lock across his hard body.

Shifting his grip he grabs me by my waist and lifts me up. Yelping in surprise, he positions me over his cock then in a single, swift motion lowers me onto his shaft.

His cock fills my pussy, hard, fast and deep.

Crying out wordless pleasure his strong hand grips the back of my neck pulling me down to him.

His lips claim mine as his tongue slips inside. I moan as he kisses me fiercely, his hand roaming over my body, while his enormous dick stretches my pussy to its limits.

His hand moves lower, between my legs, until one finger finds my clit.

As his finger grazes it, I'm gripped by wild, animal lust. Abandoning all reason I buck on his cock, riding him for all he's worth.

His finger pushes against my clit, circling it while his hips thrust into me.

He pulls on my hair, keeping me tight against his lips. His

giant dick fills me over and over as our hips slam into each other with the sounds of slapping skin.

Suddenly he thrusts up hard, driving himself even deeper, and he holds. He pulls out of our kiss, staring into my eyes.

"My treasure," he hisses, then thrusts in and out of me like a jackhammer before I can respond.

My eyes roll back into my head. Liquid fire rages from my pussy then waves of it pass through me.

"RAGNAR!" I scream, wildly bucking my hips to meet his rapid fire thrusting.

Our orgasm takes us both. His hand tightens in my hair, pulling me close and together we come, over and over. Wave after wave of pleasure, more than I've ever experienced.

Slowly awareness returns.

Lying on his muscled chest. Warm. Comfortable.

Fingers softly tracing his bulging muscles.

His massive cock, soft inside me, still filling. I never want to let him go.

I lay a hand on my belly where his seed now rests.

My future has never looked brighter.

THE END

If you enjoyed *Dragon's Kiss*, the next book in the series is available now
Dragon's Capture Red Planet Dragons of Tajss Book 6

ABOUT THE AUTHOR

USA Today Bestselling Author of fantasy and scifi romance, Miranda Martin's books feature larger than life heroes with out-of-this-world anatomy and smart heroines destined to save the world. As a little girl she would sneak off with her nose in a book, dreaming of magical realms. Today she brings those fantasies to life and adores every fan who chooses to live in them for a while.

She was born and raised in southern Virginia, but as a veteran she's traveled to places like Korea, Hawaii and good 'ole Texas. Now she's settled in Kansas, the heart of America, with her husband and daughters. Her favorite animals are dragons, unicorns and cats. If she's not writing, you can still find her tucked away somewhere with a warm blanket and her nose in a book.

Get in touch!
mirandamartinromance.com
miranda@mirandamartinromance.com

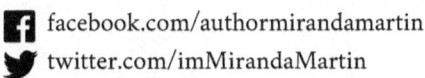

facebook.com/authormirandamartin
twitter.com/imMirandaMartin
instagram.com/imMirandaMartin

ALSO BY MIRANDA MARTIN

Red Planet Dragon's of Tajss Series
Red Planet Jungle Series
The Power of Twelve Series
The Alva Series
Dragon's & Phoenixes Series

FULL COPYRIGHT